Rachel Anderson

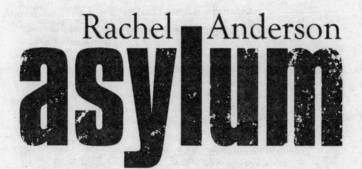

Hodder
Children's
Books

A division of Hachette Children's Books

ISBN: 978 0 340 99768 0

Typeset in AGaramond by Avon DataSet Ltd,
Bidford on Avon, Warwickshire

Printed and bound in Great Britain by
CPI Bookmarque Ltd, Croydon, Surrey

The paper and board used in this paperback by Hodder Children's Books
are natural recyclable products made from wood grown in
sustainable forests. The manufacturing processes conform to the
environmental regulations of the country of origin.

Hodder Children's Books
a division of Hachette Children's Books
338 Euston Road, London NW1 3BH
An Hachette UK company
www.hachette.co.uk

To Enzo Cozzi

Sunday Arrives

Great Britain was never his country of first choice, nor second. He'd have preferred Canada or Germany or America. Best of all, Iceland which, so he'd heard, was cold and treeless but democratic and respectful of human life.

Britain was where he ended up. After the lorry had rumbled off the ferry he waited, as he had been advised, till it slowed at a roundabout. Then he jumped down from the axle and walked casually away, as he had been told he should. He had no luggage, only the precious book tucked inside his undervest. He felt giddy from eight hours bobbing across the North Sea. Eventually, he asked an elderly woman waddling by with her dog in a shopping basket what place this was.

'Lowestoft, dearie.'

'Thank you, ma'am.' Sunday could see with his eyes

that Lowestoft was a run-down type of port and smell with his nose that it had a fishing industry. He was learning all the time. Sunday was fifteen. He was on his own. He was starting a new life. His Auntie Pru was three thousand seven hundred and twenty-three miles, and twenty-seven days, distant. He did not own a mobile phone. Nor did she.

The old woman said, 'Don't take offence, but if you're one of them lads just slipped in looking for casual work, you might as well know there's not much of that about here. But they've opened an advice centre if that's any help. Near the post office.'

'Thank you, ma'am, I have all I require,' Sunday replied. 'But if you could indicate me towards the railway station?'

A succession of trucks and boats had brought him as far as Rotterdam. There, he had been given, by the man in dark mirror glasses, a rail ticket for onward travel. This final stage of his journey to the job location lasted only a few hours. He had the comfort of a cushioned seat beside a window.

On the British train, the passenger opposite left his newspaper on the seat when he alighted. At first, Sunday did not like to touch it in case he was accused of theft. Back home, you could be picked up and charged with an offence for any number of things you had not done. That was one of the ways the militia kept order. The only way to survive was to keep out of sight.

Sunday read the newspaper headline upside down.

GOTCHA! IMMIGRATION CLAMPDOWN.
Home Sec. speaks. See page 3.

Where he came from, clampdowns were carried out at night. The first was when two uncles and a cousin were dragged from their hut and never seen again. Sunday needed to know if the clampdown here might involve similarly bewildering brutality. He was about to risk stealing the newspaper in order to find out more about the clampdown when another passenger passed along the aisle. He glanced at Sunday, then casually reached over, picked up the paper and walked off with it.

At each station, Sunday peered anxiously to check the name. If he missed the right place he'd end up in no-man's-land. He knew no one here. Travellers he had met who were also heading to Britain spoke of it as The Wonderland. To Sunday it looked dark. The sky was low. At home, the sky was high and the clouds stood like great shining mountains.

He alighted at the correct station. He located the Three Tuns more easily than he expected to. It turned out to be a railway tavern. There, he identified the gentleman who, as he had been told, would be wearing a plaid shirt. Sunday had not been told the man's name, but the man seemed to be expecting Sunday.

'Piet Ali,' he growled. It was said like a statement of fact rather than a question.

Sunday nodded. He took out the identity papers he'd been given in Rotterdam. The man snatched them and slid them into a pocket so quickly Sunday hardly realized it had happened.

'You don't go showing that stuff around like it's Christmas cards,' the man snarled.

Sunday said, 'But, sir, those are my new papers. Are you to give me replacement papers?'

'Keep your voice down, kid.'

'I was informed,' said Sunday primly, as if this were a job interview, 'that I would receive a permit to work and a new ID on arrival.'

The man shook his head. 'Nah. Not my line of business.'

'But sir, now I have no documentation. No permit. Nothing.'

The man shrugged. 'That'll be up to the big boss. Mr Briggs. Maybe he'll see to that side of things. My orders was to get your papers off you, and tell you where to go.'

'Mr Briggs? This is the name of the employer?'

'You could say that. The main thing is, don't speak to a soul about nothing unless it's Briggs himself.'

He handed Sunday a plastic bag containing some dark blue garments and a plastic badge. 'I do what I do. You do what you do. Then everybody's happy. At any rate you got your job, your uniform. And the dinky little name badge. So you're all sorted.'

Sunday hated uniforms. The militia wore uniform to make them appear more organized and powerful. Some of them were just boys, even from his own school.

'Off you trot. You got to go to Hawk Rise.'

'Excuse me, sir?' Sunday said.

'Hawk Rise!'

Hawk sounded like a bird of prey and rice was surely the cereal crop that was cultivated in wetland regions. To be employed in crop-growing would be a great satisfaction. He did not know about rice for the region he came from produced mostly maize, groundnuts, yams and cassava but he was willing to learn.

'Hawk rice,' Sunday repeated. 'What manner of occupation is this?'

The man grinned. 'What you expecting, deputy prime minister? It's not a what. It's a where. Where your job's at. You're the new man.'

'Man?'

'Nobody told you? Not my place to. Me, I'm just the local facilitator.'

'But please, sir, expand. What is the nature of the position?'

'See see see you,' Sunday heard, which reminded him of the trill of the warbler.

'Sir?'

'CCCU,' the man repeated irritably. 'Contract Cleaners, Caretakers, Unlimited. You're like security guard, caretaker, janitor man. Gottit? Okay? Other side of town. Can't miss it.'

Sunday nodded. 'I thank you, sir.'

'You don't have to sir me. It's Mr Briggs you want to sir. To your heart's content, if that's the way you feel. He's like your head honcho. And generous with it. So don't give him no trouble and he won't trouble you. Now just leg it, before I do something I regret. I got other people to see.'

Sunday was used to being jabbed with a gun when

someone wanted you to move on. So he wasn't alarmed by the verbal threat. He stood firm. He needed further information. Where to go. What to do when he got there. His father had once worked as domestic steward for a European engineer. So stewarding would have been a job Sunday knew about.

The man said, 'If you're expecting me to lead you by the hand, have another think.'

Sunday had no wish to feel like a goat in water and spend the rest of the day wandering hopelessly, as he had in Rotterdam. 'If you please, you will give me directions to reach the destination.'

The man sighed and roughly scribbled a map on the back of a beer-mat, marking Hawk Rise with a double cross.

'There you go now. On your way. You already got more than your money's worth out of me. Maybe I'm soft and I just like your face.'

'I thank you.' Sunday managed to swallow the sir. 'Exceedingly.'

'You don't know me. I don't know you. If you see me about, you don't go saying, Hi there old pal. Get it?'

'Yes. I thank you. On my way. Hawk Rise. Other side of town.'

In the Pink with Rosa and Lila

The Fairview stood on the same busy road as the
Three Tuns. It used to be a bed and breakfast for
business people. But business practices change. A
higher income could be earned, and with less effort,
from trading in fake passports, forged work permits
and the people-transportation industry than ever was
made from selling used cars, other people's mobiles
or scrap TVs, as the plaid-shirt man in the Three
Tuns knew to his benefit.

The Fairview was now a short-stay hostel. It provided
emergency housing for single girls, single women,
single mothers. Children, of either gender and under
the age of sixteen, who arrived unannounced and
unaccompanied, were taken elsewhere. None of the
inmates in Fairview knew where. But there were
rumours of a residence where you were locked in, so it

was wise to hang on to any mother-figure you had.

In Fairview, the curtains were muddy pink. So were the bedcovers and the lampshade. At least there was a lampshade, not a bare fluorescent strip light that had to stay on throughout the night like at the first hostel they were sent to.

'Pink zero,' Rosa told the housekeeper, wrinkling up her face.

'It was a management decision, Rosemary. The committee thought it would endorse the feminine side of us all.'

'Pink zero,' Rosa confirmed her view.

The housekeeper smiled. Many of the newly arrived immigrant children were too afraid to speak their minds. So it was refreshing to meet one who was always keen to express herself despite her limited hold on the language. The housekeeper patted Rosa on the shoulder.

'Never mind. With any luck you'll have your own place one day. Then you'll forget about pink.'

Rosa's favourite colour was green, whether a forest of hornbeam, or unfurling clover leaves, or a meadow of fresh grass. Her next best colour was the yellow of sunflowers, ripening millet, marigolds and maize. The village where she was born lay in a fertile plain between the mountains.

'Mamma, what's your best of all colour?' Rosa asked. She lay on her narrow bed with its dull pink duvet and filled in her tedious colouring-in book. The Welfare Support Worker brought her a new one each time she visited. Colouring in the simple outlines was supposed to keep Rosa cheerful and occupied.

Rosa realized that her mother hadn't the will to name any colour just then. 'Then I will put yellow for you, Mamma, until you feel like talking to me,' Rosa said gently.

'Yes. Thank you,' murmured Lila. She was resting on her pink bed. She had her shawl round her head, her overcoat buttoned up. She was always cold. She was always coughing. It was irritating, specially in the night. It kept them both awake and Rosa had to get up and fetch her mother a cup of water from the washrooms down the corridor. Her granpap coughed like that, not because he was old but because he had the white plague in his lungs. And now Lila also had the white plague.

They had entered this country furtively and without visas. But Lila had not thought it wise to change her name, nor Rosa's. They had come to a just and honourable country. She trusted they would be treated fairly. And it was so. At the immigration office, they were informed through an interpreter, 'You will be granted a stay of temporary residence while your situation is investigated.'

That had been weeks back. Rosa had been given a place in a junior school where she had made several enemies and one friend, Jules, who had nominated herself as a special protector against the bullies and name-callers.

'Mamma, how long have we been here in Fairview?'

But Lila could not remember either. It was certainly too long. The mud-pink curtains and the bland canteen breakfasts were beginning to seem normal.

Rosa said, 'What if we become so used to them we do not mind?'

They had recently been issued with a Welfare Support Worker which Lila took to be a good sign. Surely, no country would waste money providing social care if they weren't intending to grant you leave to remain?

Through an interpreter, Lila had dared query the length of time the investigation was taking. The Welfare Support Worker had replied, 'The immigration authorities are always very busy. They have to check each case thoroughly to ensure there's no threat to national security. I don't know what they mean by that, but it's what they say.'

Rosa should have been in school but she and Lila were waiting for a visit from the WSW. Rosa enjoyed school. There were cooked dinners, better than the Fairview food, and always plenty of it since Jules said she couldn't even look at green vegetables, raw or cooked, let alone put them near her mouth. So in exchange for service as bodyguard, she'd slide her cabbage, sprouts, beans or broccoli on to Rosa's plate. Since Rosa wasn't there, she'd have to find another person to dump her greens on.

The WSW was to bring them the latest news of their application. Rosa hoped they'd soon be given a proper home and wouldn't have to keep moving. Every change gave her a lurching stomach, like she'd had on the sea, crossing from Europe to the British island. When they'd come off the ferry, her legs had been so wobbly she'd hardly been able to stand up and she'd felt like a baby learning to walk.

Here Is Hawk Rise

Sunday followed the beer-mat map closely. He was tired but he must make no mistakes. He was forbidden to return to the grubby gentleman in the plaid shirt at the public house for confirmation of the route.

He crossed a busy four-lane road, darting between vehicles whose drivers sounded their horns at him. On the beer-mat, the gentleman had scrawled 'ring road go under'. Sunday did not appreciate the meaning until he was already across and saw the official command on a signpost.

'PEDESTRIANS USE UNDERPASS' it ordered. There were rules about urban life he was going to have to learn quickly if he wanted to go unnoticed. He prayed that, in God's good time, he would fit into this ugly landscape as if he belonged.

He reached a block of warehouses. The barred

windows made the buildings look like prisons. Sunday quickened his pace. His father had died in a prison. There had been no death certificate and the body was never returned to the village for burial.

After the warehouses, he had to take a footbridge over multiple railway tracks. It began to drizzle. The moisture clung to his hair and to his sweater like a mist. He held the plastic bag over his head to form a roof.

The streets on this side of the railway tracks seemed deserted. Yet he sensed he was not alone. He turned but saw no one. He walked on, turned again. This time he noticed a low car at the far end of the street, travelling slowly. Next time he glanced back, it had gone. Or had he imagined it? He was so accustomed to checking over his shoulder.

He was relieved when he spotted Hawk Rise. It was still far off. But it was definitely the place. A grey tower block on the outskirts of the town.

From then on, his course was simple. He just had to keep walking towards the monster until it was louring over him. It was seventeen storeys tall. He counted the rows of windows twice to make sure. He had heard of the Eiffel Tower and the twin towers of Kuala Lumpur. Could they be as tall as this concrete giant?

Each time he had stepped off a boat, he had felt dizzy. He felt the same now. Would people live so high above the ground by choice? Where he came from, every home in the village sat firm on the red earth with a yard outside their doorway. Perhaps the people here believed it to be safer to live stacked on top of each other like sacks in a grain store.

A tiny woman was making her way to the entrance. She looked as though the rain might dissolve her into nothing. She struggled to pull on the doors but was hampered by the shopping bag hanging from her wrist and the umbrella she was trying to control with the other hand.

Her jerky movements like a gecko on a wall reminded Sunday of Auntie Pru. Such an old person ought to have paid a streetboy to carry her goods home from the market. That was what Auntie Pru would have done. There was always some waif eager to earn a pittance.

Sunday pulled back his shoulders to make himself seem older and broader than he was, and hurried forward to hold the door for her. She mumbled what might have been thanks, but sounded like 'coconut and lemon grass'. That, too, was like Auntie Pru who spoke her preoccupations aloud even when nobody was about. Perhaps she was not missing him as much as he missed her.

The Hawk Rise entrance hall was dim and smelled mouldy like latrines in the rainy season. The paintwork was scuffed like the bark of a locust bean tree after the goats have passed by.

Yet despite the sadness and resignation of the place, Sunday felt a divine message spike his heart as swiftly as the arrows had pierced the side of the martyred saint. It was his mission to bring joy into the life of the ancient gecko woman, and to whomsoever were the other unfortunates obliged to live here.

In the middle of the hall stood a reception booth. The plastic screen was cracked. A young man lounged behind it with his feet up on the desk. He wore the same dark blue outfit as Sunday had in the bag.

'So you made it!' he grinned at Sunday. 'Thought you might've changed your mind. Did Briggs send you, or was it his lieutenant in the pub?'

Sunday was not supposed to give away information. Cautiously, he said, 'I encountered the gentleman in the tavern. He advised me to report here. I am to work for CCCU.'

The young man laughed. 'So that's what they're calling it these days? What's it stand for? Control Centre for Corruption Unlimited? Okay, so stuff you're gonna need. It's back there. In the storeroom.' He jerked his head at a door behind. 'Next to the boiler. Other info's right here.' He patted the desk. 'All the usual. Logbook. Panic co-ordinates. Management office number. And you got the uniform?'

Sunday nodded.

'Else you can have mine.'

'It is here.' The bag was wet, but the neatly pressed garments inside were dry.

'Better pop yourself into it then. Because I'm off.'

'You will depart right now?'

'You bet. I'd rather go back to my mum's and live off benefit. Nobody sticks this job more than a week or two. You must be desperate, sad guy.'

Sunday thought, I am not desperate. I am calm and joyful.

The young man looked at Sunday strangely. 'You one of them illegals then?'

Sunday said nothing.

The man said, 'Thought so. I'll bet he tried to fleece you.'

'Fleece?'

'Briggs and his pal are in cahoots together. Their business is one big scam. Bet he got your ID off you? You won't be seeing that again. I dare say Briggs'll pop round to check up on you. Short bloke. Porky-looking, but hairy with it. If anyone else comes by, well, it's the ones in suits you have to watch out for.'

'Suits?'

'You're still green as a twig, aren't you? Let me give you a bit of advice. I don't know where you're from. I don't know how you got here. But you got to realize, they don't want you here. The only ones who want you is the likes of Briggs so they can squeeze you dry.'

Sunday said, 'I am entitled to be here. I paid.' Or rather, Auntie Pru had paid.

'You still don't get it, do you? Never mind, you'll pick up the full view soon enough. But don't expect it to last. This tower's been condemned.'

Condemned. That was what the military rulers did to those whose opinions they did not accept.

'Due for demolition. Don't look so worried. They won't do it while you're still inside. Don't suppose your gentleman friend in the pub mentioned that, did he?' He held out his right hand to Sunday and shook it vigorously. 'Name's Jake, by the way. See you around then. And best of luck, old matey.'

Before Sunday had time to ask any questions, the young man was striding off through the rain.

Sunday's head buzzed. So much information in so

short a time. And none of it of use in approaching the job ahead.

Slowly, he put on the uniform. There was no alternative. He could not do what Jake advised, go back where he had come from.

The shirt had an epaulette on each shoulder like a soldier's tunic. Sunday pinned the plastic name badge to the breast pocket. The outfit was made to fit a fully grown adult.

The people smugglers didn't bother with such small details. At each stage of his journey to The Wonderland, the dealers that Sunday had encountered had been eager to get the business done stealthily and speedily. Last night, in the bar in Rotterdam, the dealer in the dark glasses had scarcely glanced at Sunday's face to see if it resembled the photo, let alone checked if the details of age and height matched with the papers he was vending.

Rosa Says OKAY

Rosa and Lila waited in the pink room all morning. Lila rested. She was often tired. Rosa talked.

'At school, right now before break, they are doing design and technology,' Rosa said cheerfully. 'It is fun.' She wished she was there. 'They will be finishing our windmills. The next project is about making models of the Angel of the North.'

Lila let Rosa's chatter flow over her. She did not ask what the Angel of the North might be.

'Then, after design, they will have singing in the hall with Miss Tewkesbury. That is easy too. And the maths is not hard. I know some of it already.'

Rosa knew it was the English lessons that mattered to her most. It was hard to catch up when she missed something. Jules wasn't much help. She never paid attention. 'What's the point in me learning a language

I've known since I was two?'

Rosa said to her mother, 'If only that helper woman had told us she would be late. Then I could have gone to my school for the morning.'

Lila said, 'There is no point wishing for things that cannot be. We know we have already had more than our share of good fortune.'

Rosa tried to keep her thoughts to herself for a few moments. The quiet was interrupted by a soft smash against the window. It was a raw egg. People outside often threw eggs at the windows of Fairview. Sometimes they threw eggs at Lila's back when they went out.

The yellow yolk, the slimy white, clung to the pane like a large bird dropping. Rosa got up and closed the curtain so they didn't have to watch it slithering down.

'Mamma, have you imagined what it will be like, our new home, if we are lucky and get one?' She didn't expect an answer. She knew Lila found it difficult to discuss what might be going to happen to them in the future when she was still thinking about bad things that had happened in the past.

Rosa stepped over to wrap her arms round Lila's shoulders. 'You are right. We are fortunate. It will be good. I have that feeling,' she said. This was what Lila had told her all the time they were travelling, first by cart, then truck, then on foot, then another truck, right across Europe through one country after another. Now it was Rosa's turn to do the comforting. 'One day, you will be able to do our own cooking again, just how it should be done. You will do the dumplings with capers and caraway.'

Fairview inmates weren't allowed to prepare their own food. They had to eat whatever was dished out in the dining-room.

'Did you know, Mamma?' Rosa couldn't stop herself from breaking the silence. 'Every country in the whole world has its own recipe for dumplings!' She was repeating what her grandmother used to say on dumpling days. 'And the manner in which we do them is known to be the very best.'

Lila managed a smile.

'And *your* mother taught *you* and *her* mother taught *her* and when we have our own kitchen, *you* will teach *me*! And we will have our own toilet. As the helping woman said. So we will not have to share with other stinky people. It is going to be very okay.'

Okay was a useful word, one of the first she'd learned here. People used it any time, to mean anything they felt like.

How are you? Okay.

Do you want some more mashed potato? Okay.

Are you Rosa? Okay.

Is your lodging satisfactory? Okay.

How is your mother today? Okay.

Would you like to explain what I have just said for her? Okay.

Does she understand? Okay.

She said, more to herself than to Lila, 'And the most okay thing will be the garden. There will be a garden, though it may be small. With a tree, apple or cherry, to sit under, and good earth.'

Lila sat up abruptly as if stung by a taser. 'What is the name, Rosa, of that help woman who comes to find us here today?'

They'd been interviewed and processed by so many different people. How could Rosa remember one name from another? However, as soon as she heard the distant clip-clopping, like a mule on a paved road, coming down the corridor, she recognized the WSW's fancy heels.

'Tell me, Rosa, quickly,' Lila said. 'How do you say, we like it here and we want to be allowed to stay?'

'Do you mean, say in English?'

'Yes. What are the correct words?'

'UK nice. UK okay. We like stay.'

Even though she was expecting it, the harsh rap at the bedroom door made Rosa jump. Before she had time to go and answer it, the woman had let herself in. This was not polite. All people, whoever they were, rich or poor or in-between, should think about other people in a kind way.

At school, there was a lesson called Community and Citizenship. They were told to think about the significance of Difference and Equality, and about respecting the Individual, as well as a lot of other things that Rosa hadn't quite got hold of yet.

Welcoming strangers to the village, offering them a drink, or to share a meal, used to be important to old people like Granpap and Grandmamma. But things were different now. Once she and Lila got into their new house, Rosa would make sure they had a bolt on their main door so they could decide for themselves which visitors could come in and when.

Sunday's Uniform

The length of the trousers was satisfactory. Sunday was tall enough for fifteen, but he was slight in build. Auntie Pru had done her best to make sure he had a meal a day, sometimes even giving up her own by pretending she had eaten already. Skinny as a bird you are, she used to say. That was why she had agreed with the dealer who said he knew of a city where the streets were lined, not with gold, but with employment opportunities and fine foods for all.

'Go there and grow fat,' she had advised her nephew and she had sold her best wrapper, woven with the silver threads, to pay for Sunday's journey. The first stage was in an overloaded wagon which crossed five national frontiers before reaching the coast of West Africa. Sunday had never before seen the ocean. He was awed by its immensity. The next truck took him to a port they said was known as Nouadhibou. Sunday's wonder at the vastness of God's creation changed to terror when he saw the smallness of the dugout canoe in which he and the others were to travel. It was no more than a fishing pirogue, not an ocean-going vessel. More and more men scrambled on until water was lapping in over the side.

The waist of these trousers was wide so they slid down on to his bony hips. He would need a belt. Or a length of string or twine. That would be just as effective, though he would need to keep it covered by the shirt to prevent any appearance of shabbiness. His father, when working as a steward, had always looked immaculate in his starched white shirt and shorts. Sunday went to look in the caretaker's storeroom. He did not find string or twine or rope. But he did find, pinned to the wall, a faded rota list. He read it through several times to give himself an indication of his duties. There would be a lot of responsibility with this job, keeping the refuse bins tidy, the drains free-flowing, the lift checked for rubbish. Would he be able to cope with all that while fulfilling his holy mission to do good for the people of the doomed Hawk Rise?

He returned to the reception booth. He sat down behind the desk. He practised an expression of confidence. He was very hungry. His last meal was bread with a carrot eaten in the compartment behind the boxed goods in the lorry.

Auntie Pru had told him, 'Trust in the Lord, and then hope for the best.' He retrieved the good book from where it had been tucked inside his undervest. He rested it on his lap so it was below the counter. He touched its soft cover for reassurance. It was his one possession remaining since the capsize of the pirogue. Before he had set out from the fishing port, he had bound the bible to his chest with a strip of cloth. In the turbulent waters of the Atlantic he had lost everything else including his name, his past, his identity. From then on he could be Sunday only in his heart and, so long as she remained alive, in his Auntie Pru's.

Rosa and the Bin-bags

'Good afternoon to you, young ladies!' said the WSW. She bared her yellow teeth like a horse smiling. 'So how are we today? As keen as mustard for some big changes?'

'Keen as mustard,' Rosa repeated. 'Okay.'

'I'm a bit behind. There's been such a lot on.' The WSW had a roll of black rubbish sacks under her arm. She offered them to Lila. 'Here you are then.'

Lila shook her head. She had no rubbish to dispose of. 'No thank.'

'Perhaps I didn't explain fully? You've been allocated temporary housing. These are for your bits and bobs. To pack them in.'

'Bits and bobs,' said Rosa.

'You need to pack. You didn't have any cases, did you?' She spoke loudly as if to make herself heard above a loud commotion though there was none. 'Oh dear, I'm not sure your mother understands.' The WSW handed the roll to Rosa instead.

Rosa understood without needing the loud voice. 'We keen as mustard,' she said and obediently tore a rubbish sack off the roll. She carefully put in her mother's change of undergarments, then her own, then the toilet bag they'd been issued at the previous hostel, with the big bar of cheap slimy soap. Next, her colouring-in books and the sachet of felt-tip pens she'd won at school for endeavour. And the photo of Granpap in its decorative tin frame, and finally one or two other small things she'd collected since their arrival. The sack was barely half full.

The WSW nodded her approval. 'Travel light. So sensible.'

'Travel light,' Rosa repeated thoughtfully. Not a lamp to illuminate journeys but to be without baggage.

Surely the woman understood they'd had to leave everything behind, including Granpap. Lila said they'd go back, one day, to collect him. Rosa knew they wouldn't. Lila was so tired she'd never have the energy. Meanwhile, everything Rosa used to know about their village had begun to blur, even her grandfather's wrinkly forehead and messy old beard.

'Always travel light. One in-flight bag, within the dimension proscriptions. That's what our travel agent advised when we flew to Mauritius for our anniversary. What with all the trouble they're having at airports these days, it's essential to follow their briefing, isn't it?'

Rosa nodded. As if she knew. What was this Mauritius?

'Off we trot then, girls!'

Rosa scowled. Before, she and her mother were called ladies, now girls. Lila seemed more like a very ancient woman as she sat on the edge of her bed and slowly put on her shoes.

'Does she understand?' the WSW asked. 'That I'm driving you to your new abode? On the edge of town?'

Rosa nodded. 'Mother understand. I always explain. Off we trot. Keen as mustard.'

Rosa knew that for Lila, speaking the language aloud was hard. And who would she speak it to? It was zero making friends in a new country. Rosa knew. At the start, she'd found it double zero until Jules had rushed up behind her in the playground and grabbed her arm.

'Ms Martin says I've got to be nice to you,' Jules had

shouted. 'I'll try. But I'm playing tag with my friends over there. So you'll just have to come too if you want me to take care of you.'

The other girls, Jules's real friends, didn't want to be friends with Rosa. But having Jules was better than having no one.

Now, Rosa said to the WSW, 'Mum pleased and thank you. UK nice. We happy people.' It was important to say thank you for whatever they were offered and not feel resentful if they didn't get what they were hoping for. The Wonderland, Granpap had said it was called. What did he know? He'd never been beyond the village, except when he'd been young and there'd been a different war going on.

Lila stood. 'Thank you, thank you. Very kind,' she whispered.

The WSW said, 'There *were* the language classes she could've gone to. I told her about them. If you're given leave to remain, she'll have to buckle down and get used to going out on her own. She can't rely on you to speak for her forever. It's not right. You've got to lead your own life. I'll see if I can find out what classes are still available. But I'm afraid the local authorities have been told to cut back on education for temporary residents. I don't know why

I'm telling you all this. It's not your problem.'

'Yes,' said Rosa. 'I understand. No education for Mum till job.'

'That's more or less it. In future, you see, under the Home Sec's new plan—'

'Home?'

'The Home Secretary. The person who makes the decisions. High up. It will be for the future employer to cover costs of language tuition, if the employee's linguistic skills aren't up to scratch.'

Rosa nodded. 'Up to scratch.'

The woman smiled her horsy smile. 'So your new home, for the time being, is Hawk Rise.'

Lila and Rosa followed the clopping mule-feet down the corridor. The WSW turned and asked Rosa, 'Do you know what a hawk is?'

Of course Rosa knew. It was a bird of prey which hunted small animals. There were hawks in the mountains. They spotted their prey from on high. They flashed down to earth like meteors. Rosa couldn't easily say all that. She tried to reply with civility. Without people like this clumsy WSW, she and Lila wouldn't have been able to cope at all.

She said, 'Hawk is bird, eye keen as mustard. And very okay name for house.'

Seat belts for Own Safety

Rosa and Lila were signed out of the Fairview by the housekeeper. They followed the WSW to her car. Rosa carried the plastic sack.

'You pop in the back, dear,' said the WSW.

The car smelled of dog. There were stubby white hairs on the rear seat. The absent dog must be white. Granpap had a dog. It wasn't a pet. It lived outside and was kept on a chain. It had helped Granpap with the livestock, when there still was livestock.

'And your mother can pop in front with me.'

Rosa heard how breathless her mother was. She was nothing like the pretty flower of her name. Her face was the colour of English bread.

Once they had their own kitchen, and their own plot to grow fresh vegetables, Lila would start to get better. It was hard being strong for two of them. Some days, Rosa wanted to howl like Granpap's dog pulling on its chain.

The WSW said, 'And one more thing. Can you remind your mother? The medical. Remember she missed the one before? Nothing to be frightened of. It's really important that she attends. Not just to get your paperwork through. But for her own wellbeing. She mustn't leave it any longer.'

Rosa had to distract the woman from nagging Lila. 'You have dog?' she asked. 'Nice dog? I not seen this dog. He does not come to the car.'

'Your seat belt, Rosa, if you please. It's the law of the land and ignorance is no defence. Come on now.'

The woman was always in a rush. She must have many other clients needing her to tell them what to do to tidy up their lives into the British way.

'The dog?' Rosa persisted.

'None of my other clients are as keen on dogs as you obviously are. He's as soppy as a date. But even so, I wouldn't want to put the frighteners on anyone.'

There were worse terrors than dogs. Each person had their own kind of fear. Lila was scared of the traffic wardens. She was scared of the pedestrian path that passed under the ring road. She was afraid of the shopping mall which had no windows and made her feel there wasn't enough air to breathe. Rosa's fear was the boys, not much older than herself, who raced along the pavements on their bikes shouting rude words. They did not wave guns and they never ran into her but there was always the knowledge that they might do either if they chose to.

'So Gypsy, that's his name, he stays behind guarding my house while I'm out.'

'Why guarding?'

'Haha! You never know. Well, these days. Different people,' the woman said vaguely, as if she didn't quite know.

Was she very wealthy? Did she live in a mansion? This was supposed to be a secure country, for both rich and poor. That was why Granpap had sold his cart and the enamel-faced clock to pay the men who organized the travel.

Rosa would never see Granpap again. There were others, as precious, who would never again be seen, not unless they clawed their way up through the soil. Many had left Rosa's life, through violence or illness.

Men and boys had been rounded up to fight for one side or the other. Sometimes, they did not even get to choose which. Some eventually returned. Rosa's father was among those who had not. Groups of women from all sides had organized a peace march. It made no lasting difference. There were always more men wanting to fight for their region's independence.

She asked the WSW, 'We see you more times again? When you take us at new nice home?'

Rosa didn't like this mule-footed helper. But she didn't want her to disappear either. Every time a person moved out of your life, you had to start all over again at the beginning. It was hard work. Lila had given up. 'Bring soppy as date dog. We make play in garden.'

They were passing by rows of matching houses, each with its neat garden in front. Here, the people grew flowers for their pleasure, not vegetables.

'An-Englishman's-home-is-his-castle-but-his-garden-is-where-he-keeps-his-treasure,' Rosa chanted, the first sentence that Granpap had taught her to say in English when she was so young she hadn't known what it meant.

The woman said, 'So you're making progress with your English.'

Rosa recognized some of the buildings they passed. The lending library where she went with the class to listen to a poet with a funny voice which had made her laugh even though she hadn't understood anything he'd said. The public swimming pool where she'd had to sit on the side and watch the others in the water as she had no costume and no signed permission from her mother.

Then they reached unfamiliar parts of the town with fewer houses, instead storage buildings and railway tracks.

The WSW pulled into a parking bay beside an enclosure of new cars.

'Bob's your uncle and here we are! That didn't take long, did it? Out we tumble.'

So Rosa clambered out from the rear seat. She looked up and felt herself dwarfed by the massive grey tower in front of her. Its sides were streaked with mould. The windows were bleary with dirt. The queasiness in Rosa's stomach returned. How could such a place be a home fit for humans? She couldn't see a tree, or a swing, or any type of garden. Just the dead-end road covered in windblown rubbish, then the path of broken concrete, and beside it a twisted climbing-frame, and a burned-out van without a number plate.

Who would choose to live in such a place? It must be where the vagrants, the hopeless and other worthless people were sent.

Rosa felt so angry that she clenched her fists inside her pockets. They'd been tricked into coming here.

She was not worthless. She had the sachet of coloured felt-tip pens she'd won to prove it. As for Lila being worthless, she was weary and breathless but never worthless. However, Rosa knew that immigrants like her and her mother must hide their rage if they wanted to be eligible for support.

Sunday Gets on with the Job

Sunday tried to memorize the residents when they passed through the hall. Tall and short, dark and light, thin and stout. The heavenly Lord knew even how many feathers are on the sparrow's back but it would take Sunday some time to become proficient to such an intensity of identification. These people, although diverse in shape, colouring, stature, seemed to him too similar in demeanour. Hunched in their dripping outer garments, leaving their silver trails of footprints across the concrete floor. Sunday had seen dejected people. But he did not think he had seen so many who were also so wet unless they were drowning.

Was not rain a blessing from on high that quenched drought and brought forth green? It should not be a curse that dulled the spirit.

A child, accompanied by two women, entered the building. Sunday did not recognize them. There were still many faces to learn, many names to match to those faces. He stood to greet them courteously, despite the risk of the wide-waisted trousers slipping. 'Good day to you, ma'ams, and to you, missy.'

The taller woman ignored him. The other kept her eyes to the ground. The child clutched a black refuse bag and stared at the discoloured walls. Her narrowed eyes suggested fury and fear. Her nostrils puckered at the odour of damp.

'Well, here we are, ladies,' said the woman in charge. 'Not quite Buckingham Palace, I'll grant you. Though I dare say you'll feel at home in time. Meanwhile, I'll try to swing it so you get a settling-in grant before the next bank holiday weekend.'

She made her way assertively to the lift. She pressed the button. The child took hold of the smaller woman's hand. The trio waited by the lift door.

The child whispered, 'Thank you. Okay nice here. We okay,' though her expression hardly matched her words. Then she stood up on her toes and laid her arm around the small woman's shoulders. The gesture of comfort from a child to an adult stirred Sunday's compassion. But when the child noticed him watching her, she scowled.

'Pay no attention to what the media says about the government's policy,' said the older woman. 'The fact is, this country always takes care of those in need. It's inherent in our nature. I was a Queen's Guide, as a matter of fact. It makes us care. The Girl Guides are an international movement. Was there a troop where you come from?'

The child looked blank.

'Botheration!' said the woman. 'We haven't time to stand around here all day waiting. There's a regional meeting. I was late last week. Do me a favour, will you, and take the stairs. Healthy exercise. Put some colour in your cheeks.'

The child said, 'Canteen?'

'Canteen?'

The child mimed eating. 'Where canteen?'

'Lord preserve us!' the woman muttered. 'People are spoon-fed for months. They forget how to do anything for themselves. There comes a time when you have to stand on your own feet.'

The child seemed perplexed.

The woman softened. 'Sorry, dear. I don't mean it. It was quite out of order. Please forget I said it. It's just that I've had a bit of a day. You pop yourselves upstairs and you'll find a nice little kitchenette waiting for you.'

'No provisions.' At Fairview it had not been permitted to keep any food in the bedroom.

'There's the 8-to-late just off the roundabout.'

'Please?'

'The minimart. Open from eight till whenever he closes. It's where you will find your basics. There's plenty of pizzas, fish fingers and so on in the freezer. Mr Hamid accepts the vouchers. He's good that way. He must have been a newcomer himself once. Though things were very different back then. He had to settle the hard way.'

The child spoke to her mother softly, as if explaining, then said, 'Bits and bob's your uncle. Vouchers, here.'

'So there shouldn't be any problem. And if there is, you can call the office tomorrow. Ask for the duty officer. Do you have a mobile?'

They did not.

'Look, there's a telephone at reception. You can probably use that. So it's up to floor eleven. You've got the key. The first door you'll come to. Door number 11-N. That's N for north. Do you understand?'

'North okay. Angel of the North.'

'So I'll be in touch, or one of my colleagues, probably tomorrow, to check how you're getting on.'

Meekly, the small woman and the child went where the commanding finger directed and the tall woman turned on her heel and left the building. Sunday watched her race through the rain and leap into her car. As she sped off, grit spurted out from under the rear wheels and Sunday heard it patter like gunshot against the entrance door.

He recalled an item on the faded schedule pinned to the storeroom wall. The security guard was to be vigilantly alert to every individual who entered the building. On this, he had failed. He had observed the trio but not been vigilant.

What did that black sack contain? Surely nobody would transport their rubbish into their home? Sunday should have asked to inspect the contents.

He did not seriously suspect any wrongdoing. The child had one of the strange faces that looked as if she had been stored too long under a cold stone. He had seen many boys and girls like that at the refugee camp where he had lived for two years with his Auntie Pru. Even with God trickling one or two of His mercies upon them, in the form of United Nations food and Red Cross blankets, they had an aura of loss. They had no one left to live for and would soon be gathered up into His arms.

Sunday's compassion for that sad-faced little girl, and for all the world's forlorn children, began to clot into an excess of concern for his own situation. The melancholy of homesickness nagged like real pain.

If only Auntie Pru were here beside him. Or waiting for him upstairs in one of those many unoccupied apartments. What comfortable words would she have for him?

Sunday racked his brains. There would be none. Sternly, she would remind him, Count your many blessings, boy, count them one by one. Her advice was always wise. A descent into self-pity would break his cover. If grown men did not weep nor must a boy who was posing as a small man.

New Home in a Blue Light

Rosa counted each storey as she went up and she counted four front doors on every level. So, she calculated, by the time she reached the eleventh storey, she'd passed forty-four flats and if she'd carried on to the seventeenth storey, she'd have been past sixty-four flats.

She peered over the handrail. Lila was still only on the fifth floor.

The forty-four doors were all the same so the flats inside were probably all the same too, except that, on every level, one was on the north side, one on the south, one on the east and one on the west.

Rosa unlocked the door of 11-N. It was a north-facer. The air was cool and smelled of mould. Rosa felt her insides collapse like a split tyre. Her mouth fell open and released a noise which frightened her. It was the wail of a wolf in a metal trap.

How could she live in a place like this, a dwelling which would never glow like a sweep of marigolds or a field of barley? With Granpap, Rosa had planted out the chard, the beet, the cabbage. From him, she knew that nothing flourished to the north except lichen and moss. She ran to the window. 11-N had no balcony, not even a ledge where she could prop a window box to steal a ray of sun.

She noticed a very small boy busy in the dirt. It was too far down for her to make out what he was doing. He didn't seem bothered by the rain.

Lila came in some minutes after, panting from the climb and pale as sheep's tripe. She held out her arms towards Rosa. 'At last, our own home.'

Rosa pulled away. 'So where is our garden?'

'No garden is a shame. But see how high we are. Like cosy birds in a nest. And no hooligans will smash eggs at our windows, not unless they have giants' arms! And when the clouds lift we will see so far, to the fields and the woods and pasture lands.'

Rosa saw the canal, the disused brickworks, the distant motorway. As her dreams of green and gold cultivation shrivelled, she stumped angrily round the horrible flat. Two poky bedrooms. Okay. A bleak bathroom (no window). Okay. A room with a table, a wide television on the floor, and four white plastic stools. Okay.

The kitchen was a recessed space with a steel sink, and a stained electric stove. It had a cupboard with vacant spaces beneath, like coops awaiting the arrival of animal livestock.

What could they be for? Rosa stared till she understood. These spaces were waiting for a refrigerator, a dishes and utensils washing machine, a linen and clothing washing machine, a drying machine, and a freezing cabinet.

'What use to us is that fine vista?' Rosa snarled. 'Once we have admired it, we have seen it. Finish of our story. I told the woman we needed a garden. Did she not say there would be one?'

'Rosa, you know I do not understand all she says. Perhaps she did not promise this.'

'This place is so stupid. Too many places for automatic machines we do not have. But denied our growing space! There is not even anywhere for a pot for herbs!'

Lila said, 'We will go to the market for our herbs.'

'And it is dirty! When did we last see any place so foul as this?' Rosa knew a number of English words for dirt which she had learned when they were shouted at her at school. Filth. Muck. Smut. Scum. Although Jules hadn't said those words, most of her friends had.

It was time Lila learned more English. But not those words.

Lila needed no foreign words to see how 11-N had been uninhabited for months. Why couldn't one of the helper women have brought her here sooner so she could've started to make a clean home for her daughter when she still had energy?

To Lila's mind, the grimy walls and floor were a more immediate priority than plant pots. In Lila's village, no person grew up dirty. Nor lazy. There was work to be done in every season. Even the youngest children had their tasks. Not like here, where they were treated like princes and princesses, chauffeured to school in their high-wheel jeeps, scarcely lifting a finger to help themselves.

If only her cough was not so burning, her breathing so constricted.

Once the sweeping and swabbing had been done, perhaps she could start to cook again. If the air was filled with the aromas of fresh baking, of roasting apples, of stewing plum purées, perhaps it might start to feel less dismal.

She found their food vouchers and gave them to Rosa. 'You go off to the market and fetch flour and a leek. Or an onion if they have no leeks, and an egg. And if you should see some salt-fish, get that too.'

'Market?' said Rosa angrily. She was tired, tired, tired, of being strong for the two of them. Her friends at school didn't have to speak for their mothers, act for them, take care of them.

'Indeed yes,' Lila persisted. 'The woman said there was one nearby. I distinctly heard her.'

'Minimart, that is what she said,' Rosa snapped. 'They don't have markets here. If you went out more, you'd know. She meant that place near the fuel pumps.'

Stores of that type sold DVDs and alcohol. No store here ever sold single eggs. As for the salt-fish, these people had probably never heard of it. They liked their fish wrapped up in batter and fried in fat. Lila was looking pleadingly at Rosa like Granpap's cow on her way to the abattoir. 'Okay, Mum. Whatever, whatever,' Rosa said in English, knowing this would confuse her mother. Then, so her mother would understand, she added, 'But none of my friends at school are treated like servants.' And she went out.

If only Jules lived nearby. She might've helped Rosa

find her way about, like she'd shown Rosa where the girls' toilets were after the other girls had tricked her into going into the boys' place.

But round here wasn't the sort of place that someone like Jules would live. Rosa could tell by her shoes. They were made of real leather.

Sunday's Joyless Heart

There was no lack of tasks. He attended to the refuse bins, disposed of a rat in the lobby, loaned a broom, a bucket, with a cupful of cleaning fluid, to the young woman with the angry child.

He mopped the muddy hall, polished a handrail, and identified a cockroach lurking behind a light fitting. Several of the boys at the Mission School used to catch cockroaches and keep them in empty Horlicks tins, releasing them to run races. Sunday was not among them. Auntie Pru said it was unkind to tether a creature by its hind leg just for sport.

Cockroaches, she insisted, should be swept up with a soft brush and pan, taken outside and sent on their way.

Sunday did this, before returning to the reception desk and repairing the cracked plastic with sticky tape.

Then he selected Psalm 100 as appropriate matter to uplift the heart which remained heavy laden. 'O Be Joyful in the Lord all ye Lands,' he read. 'And serve the Lord with gladness.'

He concurred with these demands. He would endeavour to be more joyful, and to serve the Lord, especially as He had granted Sunday a secure storeroom where to lay his head on the mattress on the floor. However, He obviously had an unpredictable sense of humour in sending Sunday the new identity as a follower of Islam.

'And be gracious unto the Lord,' the psalm continued with its advice. Sunday understood the wisdom of this recommendation whether he was Christian or Muslim since God was one and the same for both. 'And come before His presence with a song.' He wasn't sure that lusty singing was a part of Muslim worship in the same way that it used to be for Auntie Pru and the people at the Mission.

Besides, if he sang aloud, the residents might dislike the tone of his voice which sometimes, without warning, rose up like a girl's. He would keep his song silent. His concentration on the good book was disturbed by a distant commotion. Footsteps were flip-flopping down the stairwell. There was some panicky shouting.

Sunday heard the feet reach the *rez de chausseé*. Sunday had gathered several foreign phrases from fellow inmates in the camps. By rehearsing them in his mind he hoped to retain them and, eventually, put them to good use.

The door from the stairwell swung open. A flustered old man with the tiny pink eyes of a hen stumbled across the hall, quivering as if he had been chased by a dog. He tottered to the desk and slumped against the plastic window which cracked again.

'Mister Ali! Mister Ali! An emergency!'

Sunday's heart, which had begun to inflate, deflated and thudded with apprehension.

What consternation was this?

Mr McLeod's Carfuffle

His hair was thin and the colour of unripe mango flesh which Sunday knew could be normal for inhabitants from northerly parts of Europe. Back home in his village, nobody had auburn hair. In the camps, however, the scourge of kwashiorkor often faded a starving child's hair to this curious orange shade.

'Good morning, sir,' said Sunday, doing his utmost to radiate joy and calming graciousness with his smile.

'Quick, quick. Dinna just sit there like a dried prune. Will you no dae something useful?' The resident had a high clucking voice corresponding with his feathery hair.

'How may I assist, sir?'

'The carnaptious lift!'

Sunday understood lift, but what was carnaptious?

'Stuck fast again. I had to take the stair. That is fine

and dandy for the doon. But going up! Not with my heart the way it is.'

'Thank you for informing me, sir,' said Sunday who had just about managed to follow the dialect. 'Upon which floor?'

'I dinnae ken for certain. Mebbe between thirteen and twal?'

'That is a long walk for you, sir, even on the descent. You should rest a while. Take my chair. I will call the management immediately.'

'They're nae guid,' clucked the man. 'We all ken well eneuch how management has nae been spending what they should. That man has pocketed a bonny penny.'

Sunday was beginning to lose the thread of the man's complaint.

'Forty years this tenement has stood,' the old man went on. 'You're a new janitor. You dinna ken the truth. It's mebbe five years back those footers ceased their bothering so now the place is damned and we're all to be re-homed like lost cats.'

'Cats?'

'Aye, that's the truth. And right now we must nae stand here like a pair of stookies while some poor soul as I am telling you is trapped up there. And if I'm nae wrong, it is the widow Ndebele.'

'Ndebele?' Sunday seized upon another familiar word. The Ndebele people of South Africa and Western Zimbabwe were famous for the elaborate geometric decoration of their homes. 'Is she South African?'

'Och no. By her appearance, she's more to the Chinese way. Or mebbe Malay. But these days you should nae judge a book by her cover. Just like yersel. Dark as a tropical night, if you'll forgive the personal remark. We're all one world noo, are we not?'

Sunday agreed, then abandoned his position at the desk, clutched his trouser waistband and bounded with the speed of a running gazelle for the stairs. He must assess the situation, offer words of comfort to the victim to prevent her falling into a state of shock.

Reaching the ninth level, he heard muffled calls. On reaching the eleventh level, he came upon some rubbish strewn on the ground. A careless resident may have dropped it on the way down to the big skip.

He could not fail to notice that, on top of the heap, lay the very item he so urgently required, not a length of string or twine, but a belt made from imitation leather. In colour it was the fragile pink of the blossom of the crabwood tree, overlaid with the luminous rainbow sheen of a beetle's wing cover. He wanted to touch it but he did not. It was not his to take. He must leave it where it was for a while longer, lest its owner had disposed of it in error.

However, items left on the stairs could be a source of danger. It was his responsibility to prevent accidents. He must tidy this up once he had attended to the more urgent matter.

On reaching the thirteenth floor, he pressed his ear to the closed door of the lift. He was astounded at what he heard. Not shouting but singing.

'Eternal Father strong to save,' came forth the words of one of Auntie Pru's favourite hymns. 'O hear us when we cry to thee for those in peril on the sea!'

Auntie Pru's village was hundreds of miles from the coast, and the refugee camp where she was presently living, even further. So she had never seen the sea. But she liked to sing in times of trouble. Sunday clapped his hands with delight. What a fine woman she must be, this Mrs Ndebele. To consider the plight of drowning sailors at a time while suspended in the chasm of a lift shaft. There was much joy in the knowledge that at least one resident in this monstrous building had the same qualities as Auntie Pru.

The Psalm of Anger

Three thousand, seven hundred and twenty-three miles south-south-east from Hawk Rise, Prudence stirred the stew in the communal metal pot which crouched over the fire on three stumpy legs. It was black-eyed bean and cassava. Yesterday, it had been bean and mealie. The day before that, bean and yam. All of these were more palatable than the mildewed bulgar wheat of the previous month.

Each afternoon, the women from this section of the camp shared the preparation of the meal. One meal cooked over one fire for six families encompassing seventeen children was a more economical use of fuel than when each cooked separately. Not that Prudence felt she was a family any more, being now on her own, deprived of her last blood relative.

'It is looking good, sister,' one of her contemporaries said.

'Thank you, sister,' Prudence replied. 'It will be good.'

They both knew that the rations issued were of poor quality. Today's meal would offer basic nutrition but no excitement. The younger women were ignorant cooks. Prudence did not, however, try to advise them how the simple addition of a fingernail of dried chilli, a speck of red pepper could significantly enhance a meal.

When young people were far from home, and uncertain of their own future let alone that of their children, tempers were on edge. Keeping in with one's neighbours when they were only a tent flap apart was more important than an appetizing supper. The children didn't complain. For them, hunger was its own appetizer.

It was not the young wives' fault. Some had been living in camps for most of their lives. They had had no chance to learn to prepare food in a correct manner, according to custom, not even the staples of their own region.

Prudence kept her peace and continued patiently with her task. The stew would be dull but she would ensure that at least the cassava was cooked through and that the beans were not burned. As she rotated the stirring pole round the cauldron, she comforted herself by reciting Psalm 23. It had to be from memory for her bible had gone away with the boy.

'The Lord is my shepherd I shall not want,' she began. 'He maketh me to lie down in green pastures; he leadeth me beside the still waters.'

But she felt her anger boil up like the beans in their pot. So where were those green pastures? Nothing but tents in the dust as far as the eye could see. And what still waters? A patch of sour mud near the water bowser where people had been careless when filling their plastic jerrycans.

Her lips moved to the words of a different psalm. 'My God, my God why hast thou forsaken me? Why are thou so far from helping me and from the word of my roaring?'

Yes, Psalm 22 expressed despair more accurately. Through its words, she found herself having to admonish God for His continuing neglect.

'How long wilt thou forget me, O Lord? For ever? How long wilt thou hide thy face from me?'

And not just from her. What of these other listless people? Would the Almighty not take some part of the blame for the state of the world? Perhaps nobody else dared to tell Him. So it was left to her to remind Him of the condition they were in.

The psalmist had written, 'I am poured out like water. And all my bones are out of joint, my heart is like wax, it is melted in the midst of my bowels.'

That was three thousand years ago. What had changed?

'My strength is dried up like a potsherd; and my tongue cleaveth to my jaws; and thou hast brought me into the dust of death.'

To be hungry, thirsty and struggling against death in a dark place was now as it always had been.

Was it wrong to be angry with the Almighty? Better than to be bitter. And the heat of anger concealed the unspeakable sadness. She missed the boy with all her being. The last member of their once extended family. Which promised land had he reached? Or had he failed entirely and been returned under guard to the African continent, perhaps even to this encampment? Over a quarter of a million souls, so they said, sheltering here from violence, hunger, or a mixture of both.

The blue plastic sheeting stretched away in every direction. Even if he returned, how would they ever locate one another? It was better to hope he had been successful. Perhaps, one day, she would hear from him. Others had received messages, even mail and money orders, from loved ones over the land and over the seas.

A week after Sunday had set out, Prudence had relinquished their tent to a newly arrived woman with three wailing children. Wailing was good. It indicated they still had spirit. It was when the children fell silent and stared at nothing without bothering to blink away the flies that one should worry. Prudence moved to a smaller space in another family's tent.

She had matured in a time of plenty and was a tall woman. Her allotted sleeping place was scarcely long enough. If she lay flat, her feet nudged into the knobbly spine of another. She curled up as if she were a baby yet to be born.

She prayed for the boy and trusted that, though the Lord had chosen to abandon her and thousands of others, He would continue to guide and succour her young nephew.

The children began jostling forward, each with their colourful plastic dish. One of the young mothers in charge checked the stew. Prudence handed back the wooden stirring pole, the sceptre of power, and stepped aside to let the woman supervise the judicious sharing-out. Portions were not generous, enough to sustain a child's life, but hardly to promote growth.

Prudence had a sudden inspiration. Would the open affirmation of God's greatness elicit better response from Him than her silent anger at His repeated failures? She was not given to public speaking. Yet before she could stop herself, she found herself proclaiming some words from the psalm which she had been muttering under her breath.

'The kingdom is the Lord's,' she said in a loud clear voice. 'And He is the governor among the nations!'

Startled by her conduct, she bent over her modest share of beans and cassava. Would the European unbelievers bringing their aid here scorn her? The Muslims stone her? Or her Lord God strike her down for when He saw the resentment smouldering in her heart?

An old man at the back of the queue responded as if she had spoken the grace.

'Amen.'

Might this indicate that God could indeed see the horror all around and might decide to do something about it?

Lila's Memory Treasure

Three thousand, seven hundred and twenty-three miles north-north-west from Prudence and the steaming cauldron, Lila rinsed the bucket and wrung out the mop which must be returned to the young boy in the entrance hall.

He was a black, though well-mannered. Lila had been surprised by how many of them there were in this country, some in positions of responsibility. There had been a brown-faced doctor at the clinic she had been sent to and there were dark-skinned clerks working in the offices where she and Rosa had been interviewed. Her father had warned her to avoid contact with black people as their intentions were never good. Perhaps, she was beginning to see, her father had known less about the world than he claimed for it was surely thanks to one of those brown clerks in the housing office that she now found herself in this strange, but secure eyrie of a home.

11-N was sparsely furnished, like a cell. The helper woman had said it would be a temporary home, until their case had a full hearing in the court. Even so, 11-N would benefit from brightening. But not now. Lila was fatigued from the cleaning. She must lie down.

She had inherited the white plague in her lungs from her parents. She had not expected it to progress so fast. Some people said the white plague was a bacterial infection which could be cured with modern medicine. Others claimed it was a family curse which you would never conquer, any more than you could resist the invaders who came to seize your best pastures so they could drill for oil.

Lila was scared. What if she became so weak she could no longer take care of herself and Rosa? There were no aunties here, just up the lane, no dear cousin close by in whom to confide.

Lila was accustomed to support, even through the worst of the troubles. But here, what would become of Rosa? Would they take her away and turn her into a European citizen with no knowledge of the past?

Perhaps that was the only solution. Was their heritage worth holding, filled for so many years with the struggle for the lands between the mountains, with fighting over invisible frontiers against heavily armed intruders? When the trespassers had first entered the village from the north, Lila had been a schoolgirl. She had learned, by watching the adults, to disregard orders shouted in the alien language, even when the meaning was understood. The people made their ears blind, their eyes unhearing. Lila learned to do the same.

Here in The Wonderland, Lila found that her ears remained obstinately blind and her eyes unhearing. Language, and how to ignore it or to master it, was her main concern.

Rosa heard the English spoken all through the days at school. And she also spoke it with the officials. Quite often, she tried to speak it with Lila. It was disturbing, though Rosa meant well enough. Soon, Rosa would be fluent. In fifteen years or so she would want to marry a British citizen. And breed English-speaking children who consumed tasteless white bread, had to be driven to school in bullet-proof jeeps, and with whom Lila could not communicate so they would know nothing of their origins.

Lila recalled herself, a child, working in the kitchen where the big door opened straight on to the yard. Her grandmother threw corn for the hens while Lila and her mother rolled the sourdough. She could feel its silky texture.

Rosa wanted to know how to cook dumplings in their traditional way. She was right. The recipes of the foremothers should be preserved. Lila must acquire paper and a pen. She must write the recipes, in English, for how else would Rosa's children know what ingredients to ask for?

Lila drifted into a dream of potato dumplings and green pepper sauce, of caraway cakes, stuffed cabbage and saffron cakes. She smelled capers, candied peel, and musky nutmeg, grated from the hard brown seed which grew in the lush tropical lands where all the children's faces were as chocolate dark as the smiling boy downstairs.

Perhaps the many countries of the world were not so far apart as she had feared. Or maybe they were further and nobody ever got back to where they started.

Sunday and the Small Lady
in the Lift

'Ma'am, ma'am, please keep calm,' Sunday called through the doors of the lift. 'I am here to help.' Either the owner of the voice failed to hear, or she deliberately chose to ignore Sunday's words of comfort, for her gallant singing on behalf of those in peril at sea continued. When the last line of the last verse was reached, the voice continued, with barely a pause, on a new one.

Sunday recognized it, from *Hymns Ancient and Modern*, as 'Who would true valour see, Let him come hither'. Obviously, the poor lady had to keep on singing as her only means of avoiding panic. It would be discourteous to interrupt. So there was nothing for it but to join the musical exhortation to become like pilgrims on the journey of life.

Sunday had been accustomed, from childhood, to escorting his aunt to sessions of worship through song. They often lasted for several hours so it was no hardship to remain on his knees on the floor beside the lift and participate in several rousing verses before he set off to seek more worldly assistance.

On his descent, he discovered that the rubbish left on the ninth floor had gone but the shiny pink belt still lay there, coiled like a snake resting in the sun. It was as if it had been deliberately placed there for him to find. He picked it up gingerly. It was not new. The shiny plastic was slightly cracked, but it was perfectly serviceable. He threaded it through the loops on his waistband, fastened the gilt buckle. It was the right length.

He had not prayed for a belt, but had merely hoped to chance upon a length of string, so the discovery of this item could not be counted as a direct answer to prayer. It was more like a minor miracle, a reminder that his needs were being taken care of even when he made no precise request.

Sunday placed his hands together, palm to palm, and gave thanks where thanks were due. 'O Lord, just as you keep count of the number of feathers on the sparrow's back, so you take care of my requirements, however small. So please accept my gratitude that you watch over me at all times. Amen.'

Now that his trousers were secure, he was able to skip down the stairs unhampered by trailing turn-ups. In the hall, a lively crowd of residents had gathered to discuss the issue of the lift.

Everybody had an opinion concerning Mrs Ndebele. That she was a splendid old bird. That she'd been living here for forty years. That her husband had been a brute. Some also had opinions on other aspects of Hawk Rise. Most had extreme opinions about the local authority and also about central government. Advice, conflicting and compatible, was poured out.

Sunday suggested that the management office could, given the emergency, be contacted. 'I have the number on the desk.' He added, just as Auntie Pru might have done, 'Is it surely not best to strike while the iron is hot?'

'Och no! We'll not want to be calling on them. They're a fushionless bunch, worse than useless.'

'They could send repair men?'

'Are you joking? In six months' time when it'll be too late!'

'Aye, and they'll say it's no worth the expense.'

Sunday was prepared to risk bringing on the wrath

of management and exposure of his own status, to resolve this calamity before it became a tragedy. 'So, send for Mr Briggs?' he ventured.

Nobody wanted him either. 'He's crooked as a bent nail.'

Sunday was bewildered. What should he do? Surely, it was his responsibility to keep the place safe? Yet the residents were in accord that this was an internal matter. They were like passengers on a sinking boat far out to sea. They did not trust that any life-saver would be interested enough in this small predicament to bother to respond in time, if at all.

So Sunday let the people continue to mill and discuss while he ran back up the stairs to the trapped woman. He called to her, 'Have faith for help is on hand!' Then he redescended. He was relieved to find that the crowd was dispersing. He must now do the one thing he knew he was good at.

He sat down at the reception desk which was beginning to feel like his place of personal protection. He noted how it had a similarity to those boxy wooden pews which the Europeans liked to put in their mission chapels. He bowed his head and he began to pray.

He must, as always, trust in the Lord for if He could walk on water, could rise from the dead, could offer everlasting life, sending a few angels to assist a trapped lift-user, even if she was not of the faith, despite her singing which could have been a mere ruse to confuse the Devil, would be a simple accomplishment.

Within the hour, the jammed lift doors on the fourteenth floor unchained themselves. Mrs Ndebele descended rapidly but unharmed, to the ground floor.

Sunday recognized her as the slight creature, like a faded orchid, whom he had seen on his arrival gusted by the winds.

'Ma'am,' he said. 'May I congratulate you on your serenity of manner during your time of trial.'

'Nonsense, boy.' She tapped the reception desk with her little floral umbrella. 'I have suffered troubles in my life, among which we might count my second husband, the late Mr Ndebele. But I can assure you that a short delay in popping out for a forgotten tin of coconut milk does not number among them.'

She unfurled her umbrella and tottered out into the rain.

Once she was out of sight, Sunday took a piece of paper and wrote out a notice.

PLEASE RESIDENTS ALL TRY USE THE STAIRS
WHENEVER IT IS POSSIBLE FOR YOU.

Surely, if the lift made fewer trips, it would last longer. And that would help preserve the need for the Lord's miraculous intervention for something which might be more serious.

Ice-cold Bread and Paper Cut-outs

Rosa ambled back from the 8-to-late minimart without the salt-fish, buckwheat flour, onion and single egg her mother had requested but with a tin of chick peas, a tin of tiny fish in scarlet juice, a jar of Olde English mustard and a rock-hard plastic pack of long-life, part-bake, the only type of bread left in Mr Hamid's freezer chest.

The little boy was still playing in the dirt. He had a piece of string and he seemed to be talking to someone even though there was nobody else there. Rosa said, 'Hi.' But he took no notice. Perhaps he was a deaf mute. Perhaps he was impolite. Or maybe he was as scared of her as she was of the bigger children at school.

She headed for the stairs. She had overheard two customers in the 8-to-late warning of the risks of using the lift. As she mounted the stairs, she read the part-bake instructions.

Simple to use!
Step 1. Lightly dampen top with water.
Step 2. 7–12 mins in hot oven.
Makes 4 home-fresh ciabatta-style rolls.
Enjoy the taste of Italy any time!

There were other words that Rosa didn't know. She read them anyway. Potassium sorbate. Stabilizer. Methyl cellulose. Disodium diphosphate. Sodium metabisulphite. She memorized them. She would find out later if they would make useful additions to her vocabulary. It was increasing all the time. You could pick up words all over the place. Metaphors too, which were more interesting than isolated words.

11-N smelled clean as a whistle (one of the teaching assistant's favourites), and Lila was sleeping like a dog. Or was it like a hog? Or like a cat? Rosa couldn't remember. Like a cat sounded best and was certainly how Lila looked, snuggled up at one end of the bed on top of the blanket.

Rosa wished she hadn't been so angry. It wasn't Lila's fault that Hawk Rise was as unpleasant as

Fairview. At least they wouldn't be eating rancid chips any more, nor that mysterious meat sauce made from brown powder. Rosa remembered how Granpap had told her, 'Be kind to your mamma. In your new country, she will be both your family and your friend.'

This didn't feel like a good place. So it was up to her to make it good. At nine years old she could take on more responsibility. She must make 11-N more like a real home. She laid Lila's patterned shawl on the floor as a rug, spread her own headscarf on the table as a cloth. She hung the tin-framed photo of Granpap from a hook. She selected three of the best pages from the colouring-in books to display alongside Granpap. He would be so surprised if he knew he was keeping company with a clown, an elephant and a troupe of Eastern dancers with rude bare bellies.

11-N still looked austere. At Granpap's, although each room was bare, the wooden walls were friendly. Every panel of every door or cupboard was stencilled with birds, roses, lilies, snowflakes. Every shelf and every surface had a white lace runner that had been made by Lila's grandmamma a hundred years before.

Rosa thought about the problem as seriously as the teacher checking the class register. Granpap's face may have faded but she could see his house clearly. As clear as mud, they said, though it didn't make sense because mud was what you kept outside in the yard so the indoor would stay clean as a whistle. That didn't make sense either but it was what they said.

At Granpap's, windows had wooden shutters. Rosa couldn't make shutters out of nothing. But she knew how to make window decorations. She settled cross-legged on the shawl. She didn't switch on a light because the bulbs were bare and she didn't want to disturb Lila, resting as tired as a kitten. There was enough light from outside to see. She took a sheet of newspaper she had found on the stairway. She folded it, and creased, pleated and sliced. She had no scissors so she used Lila's nail-file for the cutting. Soon, she had created a flight of supernatural birds. She filled in their plumage with rainbow colours, then attached them to the windowpanes with tiny strips of pink sticking-plaster. In the same way, she made a bouquet of newspaper roses to display on the table. Then a lace-patterned paper fan for each of the bare light bulbs.

She stood up and admired her work. 11-N didn't look like Granpap's but it was becoming bright as a button, pretty as a picture, sharp as a needle, light as a feather.

Rosa picked up the bucket and the mop to make her

third trip down to ground level. She had been absent from school for a full morning and all of the afternoon. Would Jules have noticed? Would she be wondering if something had happened to Rosa? Or did Jules have so many friends that people came and went from her life without her being bothered?

Rosa didn't have a clock and with the heavy rain-clouds pressing up against the windows of the eleventh floor, it was hard to tell the time by looking out.

It was too late to reach the school in time to capture any valuable learning for that day. And anyway, she must start inventing a meal from English mustard, Spanish garbanzos, Moroccan anchovies and cold bread that was pretending to be Italian. She would do her best. If only it could be dumplings in the familiar way.

Meet Mr McLeod

'There was another wee matter I must bring to your attention.'

The chicken-headed man who'd first called the alert reappeared at the reception desk, clucking as if searching for grain.

'That carfuffle with the lift washed it clean oota ma mind. The licht. On ma landing. Gone again. Vandalized by the kiddies, I dare say. One time there dinna was folks so mean. I had to make ma way doon in the dark! It is nae good eneuch.'

Darkness was a relative concept. Sunday had known many kinds of darkness. At night, the village was naturally dark. No orange glow from street lights or blue fluorescent strips. Yet it had been familiar dark. Until the troubles came. After that no night was thick enough to hide you. Even on the blackest of moonless nights the people felt as if they glowed. Fear was everywhere. The militia chased boys through the bush. They sensed you almost as soon as you smelled them. The scent of terror off the pursued was stronger than the sweat of the pursuer.

'And on which level has the unfortunate lamplight mishap occurred?' Sunday asked. He picked up a pencil to note the problem in the Maintenance and Mishaps schedule he had started.

'You ken well enough where I'm fra!' the man snapped. 'Was I no speaking with you last week, concerning incomers leaving their mess on the stair till it stinks like a midden? It will bring back the rats.'

'Excuse me, sir. I was not in employment here last week.'

The man shrugged. 'Then it was the other fellow.' He gestured upwards. 'It's floor eight. 8-E. Do you have mind o' that?'

'Yes, sir. Level eight. I will be attentive to this matter,' said Sunday, while under his breath he begged, Please, Lord, let me love this short-tempered man as You love me despite my shortfalls.

The Lord was increasingly mysterious in His method of response to prayer. He left some calls unanswered for months. On other occasions, a request was settled in the blink of an eye. As now, the old fellow's mood changed abruptly as if he had been touched by grace. 'Fegs, boy! I apologize for my blethering. Been a wee bit out o' sorts. It's the worry about what's to become of us when the building comes doon. No excuse for bad manners though. I shouldna hae mistaken you for the other laddie.' He jabbed excitedly at the badge pinned to Sunday's shirt pocket. 'Mr Ali, course you are.'

Sunday hated lies. Auntie Pru said that wherever there was truth there would be concord, where there were lies there would be death. Sunday wanted to confess that the name belonged to someone else, an unknown.

'Piet Ali.' The man insisted on repeating it. 'That'll be the Dutch? For you hail from the Netherlands if I'm no mistaken in what I've heard?'

Sunday gave an uncertain nod. That at least was no lie. He had indeed arrived from Rotterdam. While there he'd seen little, having spent days under a tarpaulin on a barge, sliding out only in the dead of night to wander the streets and marvel at the shuttered shops.

The man thrust his freckled hand towards Sunday. 'And you'll know me as Angus McLeod.'

Auntie Pru said civility won the battles without the bloodshed. Sunday responded to the man's enthusiastic handshake. 'You've picked up a fine command of our ways. Dare say you'll have learned in school? Hard workers, you Dutchmen. The English will no be bothered and their educational system is a disgrace.' Mr McLeod lowered his voice. 'And book learning is not the only thing he'll no bother with.'

He propped himself against the desk as if it were one of those fancy bars Sunday had seen in Rotterdam, and as if Sunday were the waiter in the white waistcoat who mixed the cocktails.

'I'm no fra England, you understand. I first saw the light o' day in Aberdeen, the Granite City we call it for oor fine buildings sparkle like black diamonds. But ma faither was an engineer. Africa is where I grew up. It was a fine life. That'll be why I respond so well to you. My first nursemaid was dark as you. I knew her face better than I knew ma ain mither's.'

Sunday, though no bartender, nonetheless recognized a lonely soul whose worries of darkness and rats were only a cover. What he needed was stories of other men's misfortunes to lift him from his isolation.

Auntie Pru told stories. When a man's heart is sad, she said, strong drink is all very well but what he truly needed was prayer followed by the solace of a good story from the old testament or the new.

Sunday, too, was lonely and he had a story that he yearned to tell. How his family's peaceful life had been destroyed, first by the droughts, and then by the new government's raiding parties. His brothers disappeared. Then his father was captured, later his mother too. Sunday went to live with his aunt until her home was no longer safe. Together, they had fled to their last hope, the refugee camp. There, starvation was kept at bay but every day lasted a hundred years and was as relentlessly purposeless as the one before. It was from the camp that Sunday had eventually set out in a group of boys and young men on the hazardous quest to find new lives.

Sunday was the past and all his experiences must be kept close as an oyster.

'Please, Lord, bring me comfort. Please, Lord, feed me with the bread of life.'

Sunday Prays

When idle, he thought too much about the past. He remembered his earliest years in the village. Desertification had already begun. Crops failed. The dunes moved ever closer, at several metres a year. Two lakes were swallowed by the sand. Sunday remembered the arrival of the climatologists in their Land-Rover with all their equipment. As friction between the political groups increased, foreign scientists no longer came to measure the dunes. Nobody came, except the warlords and militia.

That was a bad time, better to erase it. He turned his thoughts instead to his aunt. Her dear face was clear. He could see the skin worn shiny like an old leather purse. He saw the creases in her cheeks. Her huge moist eyes drooped with a lifetime's sorrow but then her smile broke through like a betel nut cracking from the shell.

She had been the eldest of fourteen. Sunday's father had been among the youngest. Of that generation, only Auntie Pru was left.

In the dim storeroom next to the boiler, he knelt, placed his palms together and prayed. 'Dear Lord, if it is your will, keep Aunt Prudence safe from harm. And also dear Lord, if it is also your will, maintain her in good health until I have found security here, and true papers, and good money to buy us a nice big house with a yard and then I can send her the air ticket and she will join me in this dark but pleasant land. Amen.'

There was no need to pray for his father or mother. They were already safe in the arms of Jesus.

Prudence Broods

Where was the boy now? Who was caring for him? Had he fallen among thieves and evil-doers who would drag him down to their base level or was he settled amongst good companions who would lead him along paths of righteousness? Was he eating, remembering to say his prayers?

Entrusting his welfare to the mercy of the Lord had been the correct thing to do. But it did not prevent the uncertainty from gnawing into her. She wanted her heart put at rest. The latest rumour to circulate the camp was vexing.

A group of young fishermen, the reports said, had set out from Senegal. They had sailed nearly as far as the Canary Islands before a storm capsized them. Many drowned, so the story went, but there were survivors who were being held by the Spanish in a camp on the island of Fuerteventura. Could it be that Sunday had passed through six frontiers to reach the coast, that he had befriended a group of fishermen and gained a place on their doomed vessel?

When, by day, she saw the misery around her, she was glad that he had escaped, even if it was to lie in the waters of the deep. At night, she soothed herself with pleasant visions of her village and she forgot why they had had to leave. She imagined the branches of the mango casting a welcome pool of shadow in the compound. She heard the cockerel strutting grandly through the fallen fruits. She listened to the cheerful chatter of her neighbours and the lively shouts of children skipping to school. She imagined herself rising from a snooze and setting out with the other women to the borehole for water.

An arduous life before the troubles, yet an honourable one.

Sunday, Servant to the People

He had asked for heavenly assistance for this work. His prayer was answered. When there was much to do, there was less worry. Residents came seeking whatever small thing they had a sudden whim for. Mrs Roberts from 14-E wished to bake a Victoria sponge and came asking to borrow a vanilla pod. Sunday had no such thing. However, when Mr Diouf, 16-S, wanted the loan of a darning needle, Sunday was able to refer him to Mrs Roberts, a true homemaker who, it transpired, owned needles of many sizes. The small boy from the seventeenth level showed Sunday his tiny tooth, as shiny as a pearl, which had, apparently, just become loose in the child's mouth and fallen out. The boy seemed to be requesting a container in which to place his tooth, though he said nothing. Sunday found him an empty matchbox. The child trotted away.

Then Mrs Tha, 2-N, requested a piece of sticking-plaster. Sunday checked in the first-aid box but there was none. Mr McLeod wondered if Mr Ali had the *Evening Echo* and if so, could he have a quick glance to check the racing results. Since Auntie Pru did not condone betting or gambling, Sunday was glad that he had no evening paper.

He was, however, reassured by the many requests that his mission was a necessary one and did his best to respond in a positive and caring manner.

Naturally, there were grumbles too. The erratic heating of the tap water. The accumulation of debris in the parking bay. The television masts on the rooftop rattling in the wind. The return of rats and roaches.

These people were accustomed to the soft living in The Wonderland. It must be a hardship for them when their comforts became unreliable. However, Sunday knew it was not his place to remind them that two-thirds of the world's people had never had regular water or electric lights. It was his role to love them and listen to their complaints.

Mrs Ndebele, tottering back from the 8-to-late, asked Sunday to help her insert the new battery into her hearing-aid and, while he did so, informed him that the rats were not ordinary rodents but a new generation of super-rat.

'I have seen it on the television. Resistant to poison. I chased one with a broom. It fought back as viciously as the late Mr Ndebele when I requested he leave. It ate the bristles off the broom.' She cackled cheerfully.

Sunday said, 'But from where do these rodents originate? I am keeping this place clean as I can.'

'Off the boats at all the ports. Dover, Gravesend, Liverpool. You name it. They tiptoe down the mooring ropes when nobody's looking, and they're in! No passport control for them!' She winked at him. He returned her hearing-aid.

'You aren't such a bad lad, are you?' she said.

'Thank you, Ma'am.'

'A bit wet behind the ears. Mrs Zaid says you're like our own welfare worker. And a good deal less trouble than going down to that People's Advice Bureau. Those young women, so busy talking, they've no time for us old citizens.'

'Ma'am, I am in sorrow to hear this.'

'I never bother with them now. None of my problems can be solved by some juvenile administrator. I trust in the Lord and I respect the spirits of my ancestors.'

The heathen custom of Ancestor Worship did not

merit Auntie Pru's approval any more than gambling. So Sunday said nothing.

After Mrs Ndebele had shuffled off, Mr Johnson, of 16-E, approached Sunday furtively as a land-crab and whispered, 'Can you read, laddie?'

'Yes, sir.'

'Please read this for me.' He pushed a letter at Sunday. It was handwritten and looked personal.

'I deduce, from the postage stamp,' said Sunday, 'that this was posted in Australia.' It turned out to be from Mr Johnson's estranged daughter in Perth. Sunday read it aloud and Mr Johnson went away happy. Sunday was bemused. He had not expected to find adult illiterates in The Wonderland.

Later, as Sunday sat at his desk covertly studying the good book, the child from 11-N appeared.

'Here I new,' she announced. 'Okay-dokay?'

'Yes, missy. I noted your arrival. I greet you.'

'I am Rosa. You serving man here?'

'That is so. I hold the temporary position of caretaker until such a time as the building is closed and residents are rehoused.'

'Then this bucket you. Okay? You miss him? You think, where he gone nice bucket long time? He run away? No.' She rattled it down in front of him. 'So also is cleaning stick.' She leaned the mop against the desk. 'Not dry as a bone. Okay.'

'Thank you. It is good of you to return them.'

'Our house up top clean as a whistle. No more stinky. Nice and okay.'

'I am glad to hear it. It is pleasanter to live in a place when it is fresh.'

She peered past Sunday into the storeroom where he had imprudently left the door slightly open. 'That your home?' she demanded incredulously. She must have spotted the mattress on the floor and the pair of socks hanging from a nail to dry. 'Like teeny box, all dark?'

Sunday felt uncomfortable that she had seen into the poky space. 'I have another home, far away in another place, with lands that stretch to the horizon and magnificent trees.'

'Me also. In my other far home I have lakes and mountains very high. But it no good, so many bad men. Maybe you also come to British Island find nice asylum seeking?'

Sunday was unsure how to reply.

The child carried on her authoritative commentary. 'And so you not lucky. You home here no good, nul points zero. No window. No chair. No nothing. Up top, 11-N, we got not so bad okay house. Now I make cooking for my mum. Thank you and cheerio.'

'Good day to you too,' he said. Then, as she scampered towards the stairwell, he added, 'And should there be some way I may help you further, it would be my duty and happiness to do so. Do not hesitate to ask.'

The child and her mother, migrants of some type, were obviously not as desperate as the families he had encountered in the camp. But to live in uncertainty was never good for a young child, as he knew from his own experience. He added the name, Rosa, to his special prayer list. Whether or not she was of the faith, she was evidently a troubled sister in need of spiritual support.

Sunday Scribe to the People

News of the caretaker's scholarly skills spread. Soon, Mr Osman, from level twelve, asked if the caretaker would assist in the writing of a letter to his betrothed in Somalia.

'The application for a visa has been regretfully turned down,' explained Mr Osman. 'I am fervent that my letter will be written in the beautiful English language. If it is to be checked by Her Majesty's censors, they will read with ease and not suspect hidden deceits of which, I assure you, there are none.'

Sunday's neat, legible handwriting, as taught at the Mission School, had gained him a class certificate. He was pleased to put it to use.

Mr Osman continued, 'If you please, Mr Ali, you will write it most lovingly so the authorities will understand that our affection is mutual and of long standing.'

Sunday was embarrassed. He knew only of love divine. He had never read a letter of love, let alone attempted to write such a thing. But when he saw tears sparkle in Mr Osman's eyes, he complied.

He brought to mind his parents. He imagined the lovingly connubial letter such as his father, Sampson, might have written to his mother, Mercy. This brought on tears to his eyes and so he composed a very fine letter indeed for Mr Osman.

Residents began to show their appreciation. Turkish delight, shortcake, samosas, were deposited on the reception desk. Then, as it became known that the caretaker was living right here on the premises, in the comfortless, cookerless, windowless storeroom next to the boiler room, residential support became ever more practical.

Mr and Mrs Smith, who dined exclusively on battered cod and chips or pizza, on alternate days, for which they walked halfway into town, returned with an extra envelope of chips for Sunday or the last slice of pizza. When Mr McLeod ventured out for a stir-fry from the Golden Pagoda by the railway bridge he brought his leftovers for Sunday. Mrs Wieczerzak baked him an apple cake with cinnamon. Mrs

Papaconstaninou brought him a steaming mug of avgolemono soup.

A blanket, a pillow, a teapot, a silk rose standing in a vase of plastic look-alike water and several other small items were discreetly left for him to find.

Sunday gave thanks to the Lord for these gifts. He understood that few of these people were Christians. Even Mrs Ndebele's faith was a cooking pot miscellany. If Auntie Pru were here, how would she respond? Certainly, she would never dismiss them for their unbelief.

'Humans not heathens,' she would say, then do all she could to lead such people into the ways of the Lord. For Sunday, this was not possible. He could not evangelize without revealing himself as an impostor. Yet, he wanted so much to touch the spirituality of these generous people. Whether they were Muslim, Hindu, Jews, Buddhists, Shamans, Sikhs, Shintoists, Janists, Pantheists, Zoroastrians, Daoists, Ancestor Worshippers, agnostic, atheists or any other type of heathen of which he had not yet heard, he would ask God's blessing to fall on them all, and especially on the ashen-faced girl from 11-N.

What Rosa Lacks, Rosa Seeks

She wasn't as satisfied with conditions in 11-N as she'd made out to the caretaker boy downstairs. The beds were comfortable enough. In fact, Lila hardly ever got up. The lights went on and off. The cooker worked. There was a table at which to do her homework. But the most essential item was missing.

Rosa wished she had more words of the English. What use was it to know the names of all the chemical ingredients in the frozen and canned provisions from the 8-to-late if you could not express yourself fluently? If only Granpap were here. She checked his photo nestling within the shiny frame. The crumpled face seemed to brighten, almost to smile at her. Granpap could say 'good morning' and count to one hundred in twenty languages which, so he claimed, was the only advantage of belonging to a country with many, and changing, frontiers.

'It will be up to you, Rosa,' she heard him say, although his lips did not actually move, 'to profit from all the opportunities laid before you when you reach your new home on the British Island. You will encounter many different people. They will be your bridges to new experiences. Do not grab what is not yours, but take what is yours by right.'

So that was what she must do. Find what was hers by right. She would ask the caretaker. He had one of those quiet faces where you could not guess what he was thinking. But whatever his thoughts, it was his job, as he had said, to help her in any way he could.

As Homesick as the
Queen of Babylon

Sunday was wondering how he might break through the child's carapace of indifference without being intrusive when she appeared and confronted him.

'Yes, Rosa? And how may I be of assistance?' He slid his bible covertly on to the shelf beneath the desk. He supposed she might want to report a blocked sink, a jammed door handle or some other minor matter he could deal with easily. He had seen the condition of those flats that had been left empty.

'Plantation boundary limit. We have no . . .' She hesitated, as if searching for the word. 'No galleria.'

'No calorie?' he repeated. What could she mean?

She shook her head. She tried again. 'Mum and I, no high terrace up top.'

Did she mean she wanted a roof terrace? He

99

said, 'There are no terraces upon the upper storeys. There are none on any level.'

'We must have by the window, reached by the door. Where placing wet linens. Where to bury seeds. Important thing. Small plantations space for green grow.' She recalled several helpful words she had read on packets of frozen provisions from Mr Hamid's. 'Petit pois! Yes. Vegetable medley. Chopped spinach.'

This was a more capricious request than any that the adults had made. Sunday explained, in a way that he hoped she would understand, why, in his view, there could be no terraces, verandas or balconies. 'This building is so tall.' He raised his arms to indicate its great height. 'Its sides are smooth.' He used his hands to demonstrate the smoothness. 'It would have required extreme architectural expertise on the use of cantilever girders. It was constructed long ago.'

Rosa narrowed her eyes.

Did she, perhaps, not understand the meaning of cantilever?

'Son of dogs! There must be such place for every apartment!' she said angrily, then went on in a language which Sunday could not follow. Her face was no longer pale as an overturned stone, but bright as though she might explode from the frustration of being denied what she wanted.

Auntie Pru used to advise the younger women that a quiet story disciplined the rebellious child more effectively than a beating with the rod. So Sunday started to relate the doings of Nebuchadnezzar which he had been reading the previous evening in his tiny home.

'Long ago, in the faraway land of Babylon, a powerful king named Nebuchadnezzar used to dream strange dreams.'

At first, the scarlet-cheeked child was bemused and seemed to listen.

'Meanwhile,' Sunday continued, 'his beautiful bride pined. She suffered the sickness for home. So the king created for her terraced plantations on all the sides of his palace which came to be known as floating gardens for they appeared from afar, once the plants and trees were in full leaf, to float in the hot air.'

'Hah!' Rosa muttered. 'Nul points possible.'

Sunday did not falter. 'Many chroniclers of the time,' he carried on, 'reported their great beauty. Travellers came to admire from far and wide.' He chose to omit from his telling how the fabled gardens of Babylon had been created with massive use of slave labour and moved on to the bit about Nebuchadnezzar's prophetic dreams.

But his storytelling was not having the intended calming effect.

'You mock!' said Rosa. 'You think me dumb donkey! Big uniform!' She prodded at his blue tunic top. 'That never make me scaredy cat scum!' She became as imperious as any queen of Babylon. 'I not the Tweedledum. Babylon story many lies. Dreams! Floating in air! Hah! Fable story.'

Sunday said, 'Fables can hold hidden truths.'

'Fabled garden now. Here. This Hawk Rise. Plantations today, not king of Nebuchadnezzar long ago!'

She glared, hands on hips, like one of the broad trader-women who used to terrify Sunday when they haggled with Auntie Pru over the price of the yams. Auntie Pru always knew what to do. She would turn and walk proudly away until the trader-woman ceased shouting and called her back in a quieter voice with a lower price. But Sunday could not walk away. He was trapped behind the desk, defeated.

And Rosa too was suddenly overcome by her outburst and wilted. She began to whisper strange words over and over. It was some kind of mystical mantra which Sunday did not understand.

'An-Englishman's-home-is-his-castle-but-his-garden-is-where-he-keeps-his-treasure!'

Sunday prayed desperately. 'Lord, I mercifully beseech you, come to my aid for I flounder in deep waters.'

A Right Stushie

'Och fegs, Mr Ali! And here's a stushie enough to waken the deid!'

It was the freckled gentleman who tottered into the hall. Sunday silently thanked the Lord for such instantaneous response to prayer.

Mr McLeod patted the child's head. 'Now haud your wheesht, lassie. I could hear you from way doon the street. So, Mr Ali, what is bothering the wee bairn?'

Sunday said, 'The girl is greatly troubled.'

'Aye. I can see that well enough with ma ain twae eyes.' Mr McLeod rummaged in his raincoat pocket. He pulled out a red handkerchief and a crumpled paper bag. 'Now will you no calm yersel? Would a wee piece of my tablet mebbe dry your tears?' He handed her his hanky first, followed by a rectangle of brown, hard-baked sugar. He also offered a piece to Sunday. 'And it looks like yous could do with a wee bite.'

Sunday was grateful for the diversion, though he knew that to reward a display of bad temper was not what Auntie Pru would have advocated.

'I wonder what it was you're wanting, lassie?' Mr McLeod asked Rosa.

To Search for the Earthly Paradise

It was not enough to unblock their drains and disinfect their stairs. If Sunday's mission was to care for these people, like the good shepherd, he must support them in all their doings.

Rosa's demand for a place to grow things concerned Sunday particularly for, on reflection, he could see that perhaps it was not so perverse. It was a category of request upon which God the Father, creator of all, might well smile with approval.

He, who had created the heavens and the earth, then created first man. But He did not make him build a home, or till the soil, or form an army, or start a revolution, or take illegal employment as a caretaker. After making man, who must have felt highly confused to discover himself, so abruptly, in existence in a strange new world, God planted, for that man, a perfect garden. The use that Adam, and his woman bride, made of their borrowed garden was another story. The essential was that early in His creative work, God made earth, God made sea, God made garden.

Later, God the son had less time for gardens, being busy with His ministry on earth. However, He appreciated their significance. After He had risen from the dead, his very first action was to take an early morning stroll round the garden near the tomb in which he had been placed.

If the godless child demanded a garden she should be given assistance. Sunday stood up. 'Ask and it shall be given you. Seek and ye shall find. That is what is written. So come. Let us go outside and see what is there.'

The terrain was discouraging. The planners had given no consideration to allocating plots for cultivation, nor even to the need for people to sit out in the cool of the evening like Adam.

There was the broken concrete path, the twisted climbing-frame, the burned-out van without a number plate, the skip. The forecourt, which Sunday had cleared only hours before, was once again littered. Sunday contained his despair.

Rosa said, 'I am permissioned here?'

'You will need tools.'

She looked uncomprehending.

'What implements for horticulture do you have?' He mimed the act of digging.

Rosa smiled and nodded. 'Yes. I have digger.' Eagerly she pulled out from her pocket a metal nail-file. 'Sharp as knife. Ripe as mustard. This finger tool keeping neat as pins. When under-nails are not clean, worms enter the body. My granpap tell me so.'

She scratched about with her nail-file like a hen in the compound searching for grubs. But the ground beneath the rubbish was impacted and studded with bits of brick and lumps of concrete.

Two of the brothers from level seventeen crept by. They did not greet Rosa. They did not greet Sunday. They stood at a safe distance and observed Rosa prodding at the ground with her nail-file. Then they sloped away.

Sunday picked up a broken bottle and put it to one side. He tried to pull up a tangle of wire but it was attached to a half-buried fence post. 'For cultivation, we need big tools. Do you expect to perform a miracle? Only God can create gardens from the barren desert.' He went to the storeroom. He returned with a claw hammer with a split handle, a single builder's glove, and a bricklayer's trowel encrusted with old cement like barnacles.

'Number one is, rubbish go.'

'Very well,' said Sunday. 'I will help you with the start.' If he spent time with her, might he lead her out of her spiritual ignorance?

He wished he could share his experiences with Auntie Pru and especially tell her about Rosa. But he had as yet no money. As soon as he received his first pay, he would write and he would enclose money for his aunt. He knew their tent and the section numbers. Provided she was not moved to a different section, his missive would find her though he would have to investigate the safest method of transmitting the money. All mail was at risk of being opened and thieved. There were many dishonest ways of cashing money orders made out to other nominees. On several occasions, the people in the next tent had received mail from a family member in Canada only to find the envelope empty.

Sunday imagined Auntie Pru's expression as she recognized the handwriting on the envelope which she would have collected from the Red Cross tent, and then her further pleasure as she opened it and found it to contain more than just a letter. Knowing her, however little he sent, she would be bound to share it with those around her, insisting that their need was greater than hers.

Although he missed her, it was right that she had made him leave, for now he was no longer starving. He had not yet been paid but, thanks to the people of Hawk Rise with their kind offerings of food, he was fed better than he had been for some time.

The Sneaky Bullies

Rosa never enjoyed breaktime. There was too much rushing about and shrieking. One morning, a small boy tripped over and cut his lip which made a lot of blood. While the playground attendant was busy sorting him out, two big girls cornered Rosa against a wall, pulled off her coat and ran with it towards the girls' toilets.

Rosa was so surprised she felt frozen to the ground. Nothing quite like this had happened to her before.

Jules came over. 'What did you say to make them do that?'

Rosa shrugged. She didn't know.

'You're weird,' said Jules. 'Come on, I'll help you find it.'

The coat was stuffed into a toilet pan. Jules pulled it out and gave it a shake. It was very wet. So she carried it into the cloakroom and draped it on a radiator. 'There. See, I told you I'd look after you. Now say thank you.'

'You very kind.'

Their next lesson was English. The teacher told them to think of an unusual word and then write its definition.

Jules didn't want to do it. 'That's stupid,' she grumbled. 'If it's a word you already know, then you already know what it means.'

Rosa wrote down, 'Disodium diphosphate,' and showed it to Jules.

Jules said, 'Eh?'

Rosa said, 'So what is? Find definition.'

'I dunno.'

'Is from ice-cold bread Italy.'

'Rosie, you really are quite weird, aren't you? You can't hardly talk properly, but you want to know long words like that. It looks like science. You trying to be some kind of mad boffin or something? If you really want to know what it is, why don't you ask your mum and dad to look it up for you?'

At going-home time, Rosa's coat was still damp and was a different shape.

Jules said, 'Shame about that. Maybe your mum can

buy you a new one? That's what my mum would do. And she'd kick up a stink with the Head first.'

Rosa liked the sound of kick up a stink though she didn't think Lila would ever do such a thing.

'No worries,' said Rosa. 'Now everything okay for me.' And she thought it was okay until a small missile came flying through the air. The pointed end caught her on the cheek with a sting like a bee. She was so shocked that her knees wobbled and gave way. She slumped on to the radiator. She wanted to scream but when she opened her mouth no sound came out. She held tight on to the radiator like it was a bullet-proof shield. Her head was filling with blackness and flashes of burning red.

She heard Jules shout but her voice was far far away. 'Hey, you lot, that's not fair!'

There was giggling from behind one of the toilet doors. 'Alert, alert! Miss Bossy on the warpath.'

Jules yelled at the girls. 'That was a real mean thing to do!'

'It was only a titchy little pencil. It just slipped out of my hand.'

'No it didn't! You aimed it at her. You could've really hurt her.'

'Ooh, madam, ever so sorrio.'

'Who d'you think you are anyway?' said another of the girls. 'School police officer?'

There was more giggling, then the sound of pounding feet.

Jules said, 'You can get up now. They've all gone.'

But Rosa's legs wouldn't stand and her hands wouldn't let go of the radiator.

'Come on, Rosie. You're all right. It's only left a tiny mark. There's no blood or anything. Please do get up.' She ungripped Rosa's fingers and helped her over to the bench under the coat hooks.

She spotted the pencil on the floor. She picked it up. It had been sharpened to a fine point like an arrowhead. She snapped it in two. 'See, weapon destroyed. Incident over.'

Rosa went on trembling like she'd been hit by something loads bigger than a pencil.

'You know what, Rosie?' Jules said. 'I don't understand what's inside your head. But I'm beginning to think it must be something pretty awesome. And I'm really sorry about it. But I'm sure you will get all right about it one day, whatever it is.'

The Unsneaky Fly-tippers

Sunday and Rosa's endeavour to get the plot started was constantly being hampered by other people. Even as they attempted to clear rubbish, more arrived. A white car drove slowly towards Hawk Rise. It stopped in the parking bay. A tall woman and a short man, in smart matching jogging suits, stepped out. They went to the rear of their vehicle. They began, with difficulty, to heave out a large refrigerator.

Sunday said to Rosa, 'It is surely a delivery for one of our residents. I must go and assist. I will return to continue our task.'

The refrigerator appeared to be heavy. The couple were dragging it on the ground. Sunday hurried over. He saw that the fridge was not new, but rusty and had no door.

'Excuse me please, sir, madam, please.'

'Buzz off, bunny,' said the man. 'Back to your jungle.'

Sunday said, 'Madam, this is not an excellent position to deposit this item.'

The man said, 'Didn't you hear me? You no spika da linga? I said, Get lost.' He turned to the woman. 'Foreigners, don't you just love them!'

'Waste of space if you ask me,' she muttered.

'Please, sir, I beseech you, this place is not for the deposit of refuse.'

'Oh no? Thought it was. Big mistake. Council must have misinformed me. Thought they said this whole block was a blooming garbage tip.'

The couple returned to their car and pulled out four bulging black plastic bags which they heaved towards the fridge. One bag was loosely tied and the contents spilled out. The couple made no attempt to pick them up but swaggered back to their car and drove off at a leisurely speed.

Sunday tried to shift the fridge. He failed. He gathered up the scattered rubbish and added it to the pile he and Rosa had already started.

She said, 'Not okay-dokay. Rude as a horse. You kick up stink. In my country we shoot him.' She stopped clearing. She said, 'I now go make meal for

Mum. You pop up too. When you hungry you pop up for share. Bring own spoon. Bob's your uncle.'

At first, despite his hunger, Sunday hesitated. 'I have noted that your mother is still ailing. Should you not consult with her? I wish not to intrude.'

Rosa laughed. 'Is okay. I cook. I ask friend. Mum likes me happy girl.'

Dry and Stringy Flesh

Prudence continued to share the tented accommodation of the family whose language she did not share. They were joined by the remnants of yet another family, a widow with two young children who brought nothing with them except running noses and sore red eyes. Prudence was surrounded by this throng of humanity, yet felt she was the loneliest woman on earth. Even the Almighty was unusually absent. Could He have taken offence at her outburst at His many failings?

Beyond the tent awning stretched the desolate dust-bowl. The seasonal wind that should be bringing the rain instead blew up little eddies of dust. Nothing green. Even the dead trees had gone, taken for fuel long ago.

In her home region grew many fine specimens. The hooker's wine palm, the bitter kola, the majestic baobab with magic germinating inside its huge trunk, the magnificent pink cedar. Yet the mango in the compound was always her favourite. It was not majestic, nor magnificent, nor generously productive. The tiny sugar ants raced up and down the branches in search of sweetness. The fruit was not juicy like that of the Indian mango but dry and stringy, and with an oily aftertaste. Even when ripe, the flesh did not come easily away from the stone.

Yet still that tree had its uses. The shade it provided was appreciated by everybody. Prudence also harvested those miserable fruits, plucking them from the branches, and gathering up the bruised ones which had fallen to earth. By the addition of whatever else was to hand, pumpkin, carrot, yam, and a canny combination of cinnamon sticks, cloves, palm sugar and cardamom seeds, she produced an unusual jam which could be consumed with bread, with coconut pancakes or plain cooked rice.

She could see him now, just a little lad, seated on the ground, his bowl on his knees, eating up a generous heap of rice with a dollop of her special jam on top. And such a smile on his face that Prudence laughed out loud.

The others in the tent who saw no reason for

merriment assumed the old creature had finally lost her mind.

Sunday and Mr Briggs

Sunday was inexperienced in the use of the telephone apparatus. However, due to his lack of funds, it had become a matter of urgency that he make contact with management. He found the numbers for CCCU. With surprising ease, he found he was speaking to the man he took to be his employer.

'Excuse me, sir, I apologize if I interrupt work in your office.'

'Who are you?'

'Piet Ali. Caretaker at Hawk Rise residential building.'

'What d'you want?'

'I regret to report, sir, there is now a low stock on a number of essentials. It is difficult to fulfil my tasks if I do not have cleaning liquids. This might lead to a public health situation. If I had money, I would purchase them myself. So I also request some information about my wages.'

He heard a sound like a hyena coughing. 'Wages?'

Sunday said uncertainly, 'Payment for the work I am doing here?'

There was a long silence, then, 'Contract's ended.'

Sunday had not yet had any contract. 'My position here?' he said. 'Have I not given satisfaction?'

'Not *your* contract. Mine. CCCU. With that property. It's over. I told them. Now I'm telling you. I got bigger fish coming up.' Then the call was terminated.

Sunday knew better than to redial immediately. When a creature is angry he must be given time to recover his composure.

Mixed Menus

A letter was pushed through the letterbox. It was for Lila. Rosa hoped it might concern their citizenship applications. She had understood enough to know that their long-term position here was still precarious. She wanted security for herself and Lila. She opened the letter. It was typed. It wasn't from the immigration office, nor from the social welfare people, but from something called the Area Health Manager's office.

It requested Lila to attend a clinic for an X-ray which didn't make sense. Rosa wasn't mentally deficient. She knew perfectly well what X-rays were. They were what you had to have if you broke your leg bone falling off a loaded hay wagon. This had happened to a boy she once knew. It was his own fault. He'd been showing off. He was carried away yelping and when he came back wearing a plaster cast he described the X-ray machine. But he never walked straight again.

But Lila hadn't broken any bones. Moreover, she wasn't well enough to go right across town. So Rosa put the letter in a safe place to read it to Lila when she was feeling stronger.

Their evening meals were dispiriting. Lila was as indifferent to the pinkish chicken sausages tinned in brine and soft beans in their slippery, shiny, orange-coloured sauce from Mr Hamid's shelves as she was to the emerald green peas from his freezer.

Rosa invited Mr Ali to come up and share with them again. Lila's appetite was small so there always seemed to be enough. It was good to have someone else to talk with. Mostly, Rosa did the talking and Mr Ali listened. She told him about the plants she would like to put in their garden when it was ready. She wanted similar vegetables to those Granpap grew. When she did not know the word, she drew a picture for Mr Ali. She showed him the framed photo of Granpap.

He said, 'He looks like a kind man.'

Rosa was pleased. She was going to tell Mr Ali about Granpap being so sad because of all that had happened to their village. How the troubles had started when a neighbour was shot in his doorway and his home set alight by the invaders from across the frontier, as a warning to the rest of them. How the village had been gradually destroyed. But she didn't feel she yet had the right words in any language.

Besides, it was better that Mr Ali shouldn't know she came from a place where people fought one another. She wanted Mr Ali to like her. She wanted them to be friends. She wanted to call him Piet.

Sometimes he looked surprised at what was on the plate she held out for him. But if he found the food which she served cold from the tin odd, she found his behaviour strange too. He always closed his eyes and whispered some words under his breath before he would eat, then he spooned up every morsel in the bowl as fast as he could, even the little fish finger that was still frozen in the middle.

Lila, by contrast, left most of her meal as if she hadn't the energy to lift the spoon to her mouth.

It wasn't only the repetitive diet that Lila failed to respond to. She was no longer interested in hearing of Rosa's day at school, nor in their bird's-eye view from their window, nor in troubling about whether their asylum claim had yet been given its appeal date. She hardly noticed Mr Ali, that first time he came up to eat with them. It was as though she no longer cared about anything.

When Rosa set out for school, Lila was resting, and still resting when Rosa returned. Sometimes Lila kept her coat on because she was so cold. Mostly, she was too hot, yet shivering with it. Rosa struggled to be loving as a daughter, helpful as a friend, as Granpap had advised her.

However, Granpap wasn't here to tell them constantly what to do, and Rosa now had other friends. She had Piet Ali. She had Jules, when Jules could be bothered. There was Enzo, the youngest of the three brothers from the top floor. She sometimes met him playing on the stairs with his long piece of string. He'd begun to give her a little smile if she said 'Hi'.

And there was always Mr Hamid who greeted her kindly even when he was busy with other customers. Several times he added an additional item to Rosa's modest food collection. A packet of biscuits, a tin of pineapple chunks past the date stamped on the base. When Rosa said, 'Excuse me please mistake, Mr Hamid,' he winked and said something in his own language.

Rosa said, 'One day I give real money. No more state vouchers.'

'Inshallah,' said Mr Hamid and tucked a small bar of chocolate into Rosa's hand.

Mrs Hamid was kind too, though she was rarely behind the counter. She could understand English quite well but seemed scared to speak it. Lila couldn't even understand it, let alone speak it. Rosa didn't want to end up like Mrs Hamid or Lila.

Okay, so bad events had happened to Lila. But they should be shoved to the very back of the thinking cupboard until it was a better time to sort through them and make sense of them. That was what Rosa was doing because when she thought about the past, she couldn't concentrate in class. Succeeding in school was more important than organizing dark memories.

'Mamma, I know you're sad. But you must get accustomed to this place. You have to meet people. You could go down to Mr Hamid's and talk to him. He's kind.'

'What do I say to him? We have nothing to say to each other. He is a man and a trader. I am a woman from the countryside.'

'You could say, Hi, Mr Hamid. Hi is easy. It means good morning. And then Mr Hamid will reply, Assalaam alaikum. That is his way of saying Hi.'

'I cannot speak to Mr Hamid if he speaks in that way. I will understand nothing, learn nothing.'

Rosa went on trying to persuade her mother to speak

just a little English. 'If you will not speak with Mr Hamid, you can speak to me. When I get in from school you say to me, How are you? And I'll say, Not bad. That doesn't mean bad, it means okay, very well.'

Lila was unable to master even the How-are-yous.

Rosa was annoyed. 'If you do not speak English, you stay a foreigner and I will too. You must speak so we don't stay foreigners.'

Lila coughed into her hand and smiled. 'Yes, my little treasure,' she said, though not in English.

The language in which Rosa replied to her mother was a mixture of the old, with new English phrases tossed in like pickled capers in a salad. 'Well, I'm busy as a bee, jumpy as a flea right now. And I got scoot. So it's Mexican-style pizza with pineapple and sweetcorn tonight, all right? So see you around, Mum.'

Sunday Has Courage

Sunday telephoned the CCCU office. This time a woman's voice, quite light, responded. Sunday explained the nature of his call. How he had no money of his own. How he understood that he could not expect to receive payment for his work, but he needed a small amount of cash.

'This is not for foolish luxuries but to purchase essential items in order to maintain a basic level of hygiene in the communal areas of the building. I can foresee deterioration may lead to a public health situation.'

'Oh, that's really worrying for you!' the voice said soothingly. 'To be running out of your Jeyes Fluid and so on. I quite agree. You wouldn't want people to start falling sick. And you've got a lot of senior citizens living up there, haven't you? Old folk are so susceptible.

They'd be better off moving into sheltered housing right away, wouldn't they?'

Sunday said, 'There are residents of all ages.'

'Never mind, dear, cleanliness is next to Godliness, so they say. But no, I'm sorry, Mr Briggs is currently out of the office and your property is no longer his concern. But I'll make a memo of your call.'

'Thank you, madam,' said Sunday. 'Goodbye and God bless.'

He replaced the black handset upon the receiving apparatus. Almost immediately, the telephone buzzed, which startled him. This was the first time he had heard its strident tone.

'The effrontery!' said the voice.

Sunday knew it was Mr Briggs.

'How dare you contact my personal assistant! What makes you think she gives a figgy pudding for your little worries? There's a great world out here with bigger troubles than ticks like you will ever dream of.'

'I was not impolite,' Sunday said. 'I wished only to remind your business of the need for monies to replenish cleansing supplies so that the work may be done adequately.'

'Didn't you hear what I told you, sonnyboy? Contract's over. Dead and finished.'

'But sir,' Sunday began. 'So far, I have received nothing beyond the uniform.'

'What d'you take me for? Some kind of philanthropist? I got you in. I got you your contacts. You got a roof over your head. Count yourself lucky.'

'But papers. I am still awaiting receipt of work permit. In Rotterdam I was informed, after I work for one month, I will start to receive some wages and good ID papers.'

'Don't know nothing about your rotten Rotterdam, sonnylad. What I know is, you turn up, as per arrangement. I fulfil my obligation to the last dot. From now on, less said the better for all concerned if we know what's good for us. You get my drift?'

'Sir, please, I beseech you.'

'I guess you're only young. But you need to understand a thing or two about the UK. And I'm giving you this info for free and gratis. This very night, there's kids all over Birmingham, Glasgow, London, sleeping rough. Now maybe where you come from sleeping out's a bit of an adventure. In the jungle. Under the stars. I'll warrant, where you come from, it don't drop to minus five at night. So you was landed a better chance than most. You got given a perch on your first day. So you make the most of it.'

The call ended.

In the storeroom, Sunday reflected on the last words.

'You make the most of it.'

Although these had come from the mouth of a man of corruption, were they not biblical in substance? Had St Matthew not reported how Jesus had given identical advice in the parable of the talents? 'For to every one who has will more be given, and he will have abundance, but from him who has not, even what he has will be taken away.'

It was not Sunday's place to condemn. It was his to follow the ways of the Lord with a generous heart. He prayed that Mr Briggs might do the same, though he knew that on the matter of response to prayer, the Almighty could, when He so chose, be playful as well as efficient.

To Dig and to Delve

'We must liberate more terrain before cultivation can be started,' Sunday told Rosa so she laboured vigorously, sometimes on her own, sometimes alongside Sunday, making a companionable team of two, shifting rubbish, and sorting it into what was burnable, what could be recycled, what could be jumped on to make it small and flat. Sunday lamented the number of empty food tins, for pilchards, beans, tomatoes, which were jettisoned when they could so quickly be reworked, using pliers, a metal-cutter and a small mallet, into many useful items to sell in the market, dustpans, cheese graters, water cans, children's playthings.

Rosa did not waste time on regretting what could not be. Even so, they made little headway. If they cleared a small space, by next day it would once more be littered with broken bricks, split sacks of sand, wood chippings, bags of used infant nappies. It seemed that the wasteland around Hawk Rise was well recognized, far and wide, as the most convenient dumping ground.

After a van load of soiled carpet tiles and a broken plastic drainer had arrived overnight, Sunday informed Rosa that, in his opinion, clearing enough space to put in even a modest drill of seeds would take more work than the two of them could manage in a lifetime.

'The citizens do not see with our eyes,' he said. 'They are not aware that this is to be a garden.'

'So you soppy-as-they-come give up on me?' Rosa demanded with a grin. 'You viper?' (She had heard this word used in the school playground by one boy about another. She liked its sharp zingy sound.)

'No. But you have your school studies to attend to and I have my duties. We cannot achieve this task alone.'

'Okay-dokay,' said Rosa. 'Bob's your uncle. I have the idea very.'

Rosa had noticed how other residents were becoming curious. When she scrabbled in the compacted earth with the builder's trowel, several people had paused to observe.

'Digging to Australia?' asked one. 'Don't blame you.'

Rosa ignored him.

The Scottish man from 8-E understood. He brought down a metal bucket which he called a coal scuttle, and a coal scoop. Then Enzo appeared, trailing his piece of string. He watched what Sunday and Rosa were doing. He took the coal shovel and began to scrape enthusiastically at the ground. His elder brother joined them and helped Sunday shift two loads of rubbish over to the skip. But when he discovered an old plastic ball, he went to play football on the road instead. So Enzo gave up his scraping work too. Their eldest brother began to yell down at them from their window way up on the top floor. Both boys ran in.

Rosa said, 'Piet, maybe we harness big strong help, like my granpap harness mule to work? I show you more later.'

After she had done her homework, she prepared a notice and decorated it with a pattern of flowers and fruit.

GARDIN ASSEMBLI. Outside.
AT climming-frame. IN EVNING.
Friday Snax ALL RESSDENTS welcome.

135

She took it downstairs. 'Now, Piet, you find sticking tape from desk.'

Sunday said, 'Please wait, Rosa. First I must read this before I authorize.'

He noted with surprise that Rosa was considering offering snacks at her meeting. He had seen no evidence of an abundant food supply in 11-N. Indeed, the meals he had been invited to share up there were always extremely modest. Yet, it was like the miracle of the loaves and fishes. However little there appeared to be on the dish, he always left the apartment feeling as though he had eaten copiously.

In the entrance hall, there was no pinboard for the display of public notices or personal messages. However, on checking through the regulations, he found no rule to prohibit their display.

He suggested some minor spelling changes and queried whether 'assembly' really was the word she wanted. 'Is it possible that "meeting" might be more appropriate?'

'Assemble good,' Rosa insisted. 'We do School Assemble Tuesday Friday. Everybody in whole big school together in hall.'

'Very well, if this is the word you wish to use. However, the correct spelling is "assembly". You should not be slack but pay close attention to even the small changes in how words are written.'

Rosa stuck her tongue out at him. 'What you think? Huh? You say I non-brain zero? I tell you, I work like pigs. Three red star yesterday! Beat that.'

Sunday held back the mild reproach that was on his tongue. Aunt Prudence did not tolerate audacious talk, even between children. But here was a different country with different customs.

He said, 'I congratulate you, Rosa, on your red stars. Certainly you may put the announcement up and maybe you will recruit some of the other children to lend a hand.'

'Children? No way. Big supermen only. Strong like you. This no game for a laugh. I done most work. You done some little. And we share garden. You need garden. You need new home. Your home too small.'

Rosa had several times caught a glimpse of the shadowy storeroom where Sunday slept. He had a sink with a camping gas cylinder on a narrow shelf, a metal cupboard, a row of hooks.

Rosa passed many homes on her way to and from school. She specially liked the ones with red tiled roofs, painted window shutters, ornate iron gates, double garages, security lights, rose-gardens in front, surrounded by lawns as smooth as velvet. Her favourite garden had a trio of jolly stone goblins holding fishing-rods beside a tranquil pool. She imagined how this home would have an orderly vegetable plantation behind, with fat purple cabbages in tidy lines, beetroots bulging up through the rich soil, parsley like strips of frilled green lace.

'You got good home some other place, Piet?' she asked him.

'My home? It is far from here, but very good.' He was about to go on and tell her of his home with Auntie Pru, of the compound, the red mud walls, the mango tree. But he stopped himself in time. He took the paper from her.

'I will attach it here to the front of the reception desk. All will be aware that the event has full approval.'

The Visit of the Benefactor

In readiness for Rosa's event, Sunday set to banish greasy fingermarks on the glass swing-doors of Hawk Rise. He had no more cloths or cleaning fluid. He used crumpled newspaper which, he remembered from boyhood, was what his father, Sampson, had used to polish the windows of his employer's dining-room in the house on the European compound.

Through the newly cleaned glass, Sunday saw a long car with darkened windows slide up in front of Hawk Rise. The driver remained behind the wheel. Another man, short and stout, stepped out and trotted to the building.

His hair was long, wavy and dyed the colour of the hyena's mane. Sunday guessed that this must be Mr Briggs. Like a hyena, he had a large head and strong neck. From his Auntie Pru, Sunday knew that this savage creature, although essentially a scavenger, would consume any vulnerable living creature, and that infants and young goats should never be left unattended when a hyena might be about. The small boy from the top floor was not about and Rosa was still at school.

Sunday must not let himself appear cowed. The hyena is savage. The antelope is fleet and nimble. 'Good morning, sir. I welcome you. I rejoice that you have come to inspect for yourself the severity of conditions here, even though they are no longer your concern. Perhaps you will be able to inform the appropriate authorities.'

Mr Briggs scowled but did not speak. From his wallet, he ripped out three bank-notes, a bluish one, a brownish one and a greenish one, which he slapped on to the desk. He turned and strode back towards his car. When the driver leaned over to open the passenger door for Mr Briggs, Sunday recognized him. It was the man from the Three Tuns. Suddenly Sunday felt angry.

'Stop,' he called. 'Do not leave. I want to talk to him. I need my papers back.'

'What papers?' Mr Briggs growled and jumped into the car.

'Identification. Your colleague took them from me

in the tavern. He said he would pass them to you.'

Mr Briggs wound down the car window. 'You don't want them papers. They were phoney anyhow. Not worth a sausage. If you want my advice, you go straight to Immigration and give yourself up. Trust me.'

The driver nodded and grinned. The car sped away.

Sunday went back to the reception desk. He picked up the notes. A fifty printed on one. Twenty on the bluish. Ten on the brownish one. These were not fifty, twenty and ten euros, kobo, dinar, Icelandic króna, piastre, kuna, quetzal, sucre, tala, manta, pula, nor any other minor denomination. Here were eighty of Her Majesty's sterling pounds, the strongest currency in the whole world.

Sunday felt that one of his prayers at least had been answered and Mr Briggs was following in the ways of the Lord with a generous heart. How mysteriously wonderful was the Almighty.

A Healing Broth

When Granpap's cough was bad, he used to be given a special soup. On rare occasions it was made for Rosa too. Every ailment, chill, sore throat, sick head, earache, stomach upset, could be cured by that chicken broth with lemon. To see the steam rising from the soup dish, to watch the small golden discs of fat swirling on the surface, to breathe in the delicate fragrance of citrus and herbs, brought immediate reassurance.

Rosa didn't ask Piet up to share their evening meal. She didn't want him to see Lila. Lila was getting worse. She was hot all the time now. And muddled about where she was. She wouldn't lie down because of the pain in her chest when she breathed. She could hardly sit.

Rosa prepared her a soup. But without a fresh lemon, fresh herbs and a freshly slaughtered fowl, she had to do what she could with tinned baked beans, tomato purée from a tube and hot water. The soup was mushy as glue. It did not bring Lila comfort or reassurance.

Rosa knew this situation to be her fault. She should've done something about that letter from the clinic. But what? Would showing Lila a letter she couldn't understand have been of any more use than trying to make her eat inedible glue soup?

Rosa became so worried that she went down to Sunday and admitted the sickness of her mother. 'Piet, you are now my friend. I am your friend. Where am I finding the physician?'

'On this matter,' he said thoughtfully, 'I have no experience. I have never been unwell.'

Rosa looked at the telephone on the desk. The WSW had said they should use that if they had problem. 'So I take this? I speak catastrophies man? Dee-dah, dee-dah!' She imitated the sound of an ambulance siren.

Sunday shook his head. 'The equipment no longer functions. Please listen.' He handed her the telephone receiver. She put it to her ear. There was no burring noise, only silence.

He explained, 'This telephone service has been unfortunately terminated. The former management has severed all involvement with Hawk Rise.'

'Please be keen as mustard,' Rosa begged. 'Mum is sick mother. Very sick. You must give me help.'

He said, 'Those with riches purchase costly medicine. Those with faith will surely be healed. Isaiah said, I will not be an healer.'

Rosa did not understand. Why was he so obstinate? Why would he only say strange things which made no sense? 'Mr Piet Ali, you are a zero zero! Worse than. With you I waste the breath. You are now a null points.' People had said that to her at school. At first she hadn't known what it meant, apart from being some type of insult.

A long-legged resident crossed the entrance hall, talking into his mobile phone. He nodded a greeting towards the reception desk and went out, still chatting.

Rosa knew what to do. 'For the sake of pigs!' she yelled at Sunday and rushed after the man. 'Freeze, at once you!' she called.

The man walked fast. He was well past the chain-link enclosure of new cars. When she caught up with him, she ducked round in front so he was forced to stop.

He looked annoyed to have his way blocked. 'Listen, I got a job to do. On night shift. So you just toddle off home like a good girl.' He spoke into his mobile. 'No, not you Gerry. Sorry about that. Just some grizzling kid here. Dunno. Sort of prank. I'll get back to you.'

Rosa clutched hold of the man's pocket to prevent his escape. He slapped at her hand. 'Hey, hey, none of that, thank you.'

'But pleased, sir, to make my day with speedy assistance.'

'So what's up? You running away from the long arm of the law or summat?'

'Physician,' Rosa said. 'Please, I plead. Area Health Manager. My mum well out of order.'

'Poorly you mean?'

Rosa nodded. They were definitely not rich. 'Spot on,' she said. 'We put Red Cross in the picture very fast.'

'Emergency services? Is that what you're after?'

Rosa nodded. She had learned an effective new phrase. 'Emergency service.'

'Why didn't you say so? Okay. Keep your hair on. Look, I'll do it. Just this once. So long as this isn't some stupid prank. Or you're really for it.'

Rosa didn't know what stupid prank was. 'Please, emergency service physician.' At least she knew she'd got that right.

The man dialled, waited, then spoke into his mobile. 'Yes, ambulance. Yes. No. Yes. Name's Brown. No, not for me, or my next of kin. Definitely not. I'm just making the call. Hawk Rise. No, no hoax. Well, it better not be.'

Rosa realized a hoax must be a mean trick. 'No hoax,' she said firmly.

Such Gifts They Bring

Into Prudence's tent, formerly so orderly and calm, the young widow's children introduced serious infection. Dark red blotches appeared on their faces, then spread over their bodies. The children of the other family caught the streaming eyes and noses. Soon they too would develop the fever and then the rash.

Measles, Prudence knew, was not necessarily fatal if the child was not already weakened by some other sickness. There was little that could be done except make them drink water, protect their eyes from light and keep other children away. The suffering made Prudence angry. It was unnecessary. Long ago, she had seen children die during an epidemic but these days, there were inoculations available to protect against such scourges. Why were the new mothers ignorant of such benefits?

She prayed for the children. She helped the mothers to fetch their water. She tried not to rage against the Almighty.

Arrival of the Cavalry

Lila thought she was probably alone, yet did not know where. It was like the night, an orange glow from outside. Was it men torching another barn?

She called out. 'Shoot me, but do not burn me alive, I beg of you!'

No reply. So was she under arrest? No, for if she was in a cell, they would not have given her a pillow, nor decorated the windows with paper cut-outs of lilies, peonies, peacocks. These were the images that were on the doors of her parents' kitchen dresser. Now they were on the glass panes. Had her father decided to change things?

Rosa went up and waited on the landing. She heard the whine of the wind in the masts on the rooftop, the hum of the lorries on the ring road, then the distant

149

siren, growing more insistent. It stopped. It had arrived. It was very quick.

She heard the paramedics chatting as they came jogging up. They must be fit. They weren't even panting.

'This the one then?'

'Level eleven, bloke downstairs said.'

'Let's hope she's not an eighteen-stoner.'

'If she is, I'll be risking the lift.'

'No way. You've seen what they said in the paper about this place! Going to rack and ruin.'

Rosa leaned over the metal handrail to greet them.

'Hi there, pet.' One of them waved back.

'So now no more worries for me,' said Rosa.

'That's right. Cavalry's here.'

'So pop this way please.' Rosa pointed them towards the open door of 11-N. 'She is here. You will be kind. On the bed you find her.'

'Rightio, dear.'

'Matter of fact,' said the other to his colleague, 'isn't that where we usually find them? On the bed?'

They both smiled. 'Unless they're under the table!'

Rosa knew they were trying to be friendly but she had no answers for the string of questions they asked.

'Anything like this happened before?'

'Has she any pain?

'Abdo pain? Any pain at all?'

'Any allergies?'

'Any history of mental health?'

'Name of your mum's jeepee, pet? D'you happen to know?'

'Jeepee?' Rosa queried.

'Doctor? Physician? On any medication, is she?'

Rosa fetched the letter about the X-ray at the clinic and gave it to them.

'Well done, pet. That's just the ticket.'

'Just the ticket,' Rosa repeated.

Lila blinked as a light shone in on to her face from the passage. A figure was moving in the doorway. Then another. In bright green uniform. Uniforms were rarely to be trusted. They came towards her. Who were they? She closed her eyes. If they carried weapons she did not wish to know. There was a time when uniformed personnel entered the house and asked questions. Lila gave wrong answers and was hit. They smashed the cupboards and the crockery. They took some of the people away.

A third person came in. It looked like her mother, same hair, same profile, but now shrunk small into a child. It was Lila's daughter. How could she have been so mistaken?

Lila whispered, 'Who are these people?'

'Emergency service.'

'I do not know them. Are they your friends?'

'No, Mamma, but they are kind people. They have come to fetch you, and make you well. I am sorry I could not care for you enough. A man downstairs knew what to do. He was kind.'

Lila remembered. She and Rosa had come to The Wonderland, on her father's instruction, where, so he said, there would be no violence and the healthcare was the best in the whole world, except for the USA but there you had to pay while here it was free. They would cure her of the white plague in her lungs with their miracle drugs.

Her father had not known that, on reaching The Wonderland, there would be so many questions asked. What is the purpose of your visit? How long do you intend to stay? Do you have relatives here?

When an interpreter was present, she understood well enough. But often no interpreter was available and then it was up to Rosa. A child of her age should not have to take on so much responsibility.

Other people asked other questions in a softer

way. Your child, is she okay? Does she feel more secure now? Would you be happy to talk about what happened before you came here? Or would that be too difficult? You don't like to talk about it, no? If at any time you feel you need to talk about any of the issues that have affected you, then we could link you in to the services. Is that all right? Do you understand?

These people in matching green asked no such questions. They smiled, they gave their names, they wrapped her in a blanket.

She was lifted on to a carrying chair. Straps were secured around her. She could not escape. She had to trust these people in their matching dungarees. When they picked up the chair, Lila felt she was flying across the room. But it was not unpleasant.

Rosa held the door for them. Lila reached for Rosa's hand. She whispered, 'If they take me away, what will you do?'

'I will eat my dinner, Mamma. Baked bean soup. You said it was no good for you but for me it is fine and nourishing.'

'Where will you go?'

'Nowhere, except to the school, and I will always come straight back and stay here and be safe. It is a good home and you made it nice and the carpet is not smelly.'

'Who will take care of you?'

'I will take care of myself. You know I always do.'

One of the people asked Rosa something. Perhaps it was the same question that Lila had just asked. But it was in English so how could Lila know? Whatever it was, Rosa's reply seemed to satisfy them.

Lila knew that once she recovered from the white plague, she too must make a real effort to learn the English language.

As they started down the stairs, Lila said in English to the people carrying her, 'UK very nice. We okay. You very nice. We very nice.' It was a start.

Visitors

Two men in smart dark suits came to Hawk Rise. They were looking for a missing person. Each carried a briefcase. Each had an ID card on a chain dangling from his neck. The reception desk was unmanned. Sunday was on the seventh floor seeing to Mrs Swaniji's window catches.

Mrs Ndebele was on her way back to the 8-to-late. She had forgotten the tin of mango she needed for her sweet-sour rujak. Fresh would be tastier. But how could Mr Hamid afford to stock real fruit?

The taller of the men showed his ID to Mrs Ndebele and asked if she knew the whereabouts of a Mr Piet Ali.

Mrs Ndebele shook her head. 'Never heard of him, dear. Sorry.'

'We believe he may have various aliases,' said the

shorter man. He produced a printed sheet and read off a list of names like a school register.

'That's a lot of people you're looking for, dear. I've lived in this place forty years. I should know who's here.'

'We need to speak with him. There is some irregularity with his coding.'

The other smart suit said, 'If it's not rectified now it could affect his rights. You wouldn't want him to go missing out on what's his.'

The taller one began to explain to Mrs Ndebele about withholding information, infringements to national security and the new penalties for sheltering those who had outstayed their visitor's visa. With a nippy flick of the tiny switch on her hearing-aid, Mrs Ndebele selected to be momentarily deafer than she need be.

'We wish to find him. We must speak with him.'

'What's that, dear?' Mrs Ndebele switched her hearing-aid back on.

'You know where we're from. Here's our number.'

'It doesn't matter to me where you're from, lovey. If they're not here, they're not here. Whoever they are. And it's none of my business to go looking for the people that you've mislaid.'

She had long since deduced that the young lad on reception was no more Piet Ali than she was. However, who he might be and from where, neither she nor her neighbours had yet worked out. On one thing, they were agreed. Young men didn't care to be fussed over. Therefore, though they should keep an eye on him, their support should be unobtrusive.

None of the residents were well off but many were managing to offer their caretaker a bit of this and a bit of that so he wouldn't starve. Several also gave small bits and pieces to make his hidey-hole more homely.

To Mrs Ndebele, he seemed a fine and honest lad, even if he was an illegal, and worthy of their care, not like that trickster, the late Mr Ndebele, who had only married her for her passport with its lovely embellishment of a golden lion and unicorn on the cover.

When Mr Ndebele died, he'd left her penniless and with a load of his debts. Since he'd only got his passport on account of marriage to her, she'd considered selling it. But that devil in the Three Tuns was so crooked, like as not he'd have bought if off her for a tenner, sold it on for a couple of hundred and then denounced her to the authorities who would have come sniffing around, just like these two were now seeking out the young lad.

'Tell Mr Ali when you see him, that we *will* be back,' said the taller of the smart suits. 'Have no doubt about that.'

'Good day to you, my dears,' said Mrs Ndebele, waving her floral umbrella at them to make out she was dafter than she was.

As soon as the investigators left the building, she tottered for the stairs. It was time that somebody warned the lad.

Friends in Need

Rosa wanted to share the worry of what had happened. But who with? Who would listen but not interfere and tell her what she must do? She went out on to the stairwell and slowly climbed to the top floor. She went to Enzo's door. The wood was splintered down the middle as if the beanstalk giant had bashed it with his mighty axe.

Enzo was far too young to understand her problem. But maybe his mother would offer comfort? She was about to knock when she heard shouting inside. It was the eldest boy, the one who always scowled. Rosa couldn't tell if the shouting was anger or just play.

She went away quickly. She must not seem to be spying. Far below, she heard the soft reassuring shuffle of the black velvet slippers and the tap-tap of the flowery umbrella which Mrs Ndebele used as a walking stick.

She ran down the stairs towards Mrs Ndebele.

'Hello there, ducky!'

'Mrs Ndebele?'

'That's me, ducky, though I'd rather I went by another name. I say, ducky pet, you look a bit peaky. You all right?'

'I am okay top dog. But.'

''Course you are, petal-flower. Made of strong stuff. Wish I could borrow a drop of your energy. I seen you working away outside clearing rubbish. So I just popped down to Mr Hamid's for my tinned mango when I heard that siren. I said to Mr Hamid, Who can that be for?'

'Yes, emergency services,' Rosa agreed, and here was her chance to share, to explain how it was the visit of emergency services that had brought on the hurt inside her heart. But were there words in any language to describe invisible burns of guilt and loss?

Mrs Ndebele chattered on. 'I wondered if it wasn't coming for me! I could pop off anytime. Strange, that, going to bed, not sure if you'll wake up in the morning. Everything's in order. I've chosen the hymns. Your pal, Piet, as he calls himself, he's a lovely singer. I hope he'll sing at my funeral. It's him I'm looking for. I got a message for him.'

'You pop message here. I have paper,' Rosa suggested. 'I run down and I leave him on desk?'

'Best not, dearie. It's a private matter. You know, dear, we really shouldn't hang about in this draughty stairwell. It's not healthy.'

'I want . . .' Rosa tried again to see if she had words. 'I was wanting. I am need . . .' But she realized that, unlike Piet who had next to nothing, not even any windows to look out of, she had so much, including a mother who loved her and needed her daughter to be strong during her absence.

'Forgive me, petal, for nattering on. Sometimes I do miss the company. We'd both better be getting on. And if there's anything you or your mother need, why you only have to ask, don't you? A friend in need is a friend indeed. That's what they say.'

'Mrs Ndebele, thank you. Very nice kind.'

Mrs Ndebele intercepted Sunday with the spanner and monkey-wrench on the stairs.

'You've had visitors, lovey,' she said.

Sunday was surprised for surely he knew nobody beyond his flock here and Mr Hamid. But then his heart leaped. Could a neighbour from home have traced him? He wanted to love the people here, but he missed people who knew his ways, his jokes, his life.

Or was it was one of the survivors from the pirogue who'd also made it to The Wonderland? In their fear as they floundered in the water, clinging to splintered timber, to empty water cans, to any passing swirl of flotsam, they had shared many secrets. Or perhaps one of the boys he had befriended in the detention camp on the Spanish island?

The chances were slim. It would take more than a thousand coincidences and a hundred miracles to be reunited with any of them. With a slowing of his excited heartbeat, he remembered the sole person in all of The Wonderland who knew where he was. The dealer in the Three Tuns.

'Thank you, Mrs Ndebele. There is a gentleman acquaintance with whom I have not made contact for some time.'

'There was the two of them,' said Mrs Ndebele.

'His spouse?' said Sunday. 'He would perhaps bring his wife.' The lie sprang from Sunday's lips like a poisoned watermelon pip. That first lie, concerning his age, to the captain of the pirogue in the port of Nouadhibou, must have been breeding inside his mouth like a mosquito in a swamp. He was humiliating himself. He had sunk so low he was deceiving this precious old soul he was supposed to be caring for.

'Thank you, ma'am, for the information,' he said. 'Now I must continue with my tasks.'

Mrs Ndebele was frail but persistent. That was how she had kept the late Mr Ndebele out of his difficulties with the law. She went down after Sunday, though more slowly. By the time she caught up with him in the hall, he was vigorously swabbing the floor.

'Listen, lovey,' she said. 'If you're in any kind of trouble, you only have to say the word. I'll do what I can to help. If it's cash or whatever. And if it's something a bit more complex, well, I do know my way around the system.'

'Thank you, madam.' Sunday busied himself with re-wringing the mop.

Mrs Ndebele would not let the subject drop. She followed the pathway of cleanliness he was making. 'You've been looking troubled, son. A trouble shared, a trouble halved. A community helps each other. I know we can't help you with all the cleaning and the mending and that. I don't have the stamina. Mr McLeod is a clumsy old fool. And none of us have the taste for it like you. But I think I speak for a good many of us. We'll help in any other way we can.'

'Yes, ma'am. Now please excuse me. I must refresh the water in the bucket.'

P. Smith Ponders

The dog-owning WSW, whose name neither Lila nor Rosa could ever remember, visited Hawk Rise many days later than she had implied that she would.

There had been an emergency. Five Chinese illegals had gone missing between Felixstowe and Croydon. They'd been put on a train without an escort. Two of them were known to be teenage girls. They were considered to be at risk. They were probably terrified. The two girls had to be located before they disappeared into slavery or worse.

At Hawk Rise, she was disappointed to find a handwritten 'out-of-order' note still taped to the door of the lift. It was inexcusable what people had to put up with when they were bottom of the social heap. Just suppose one of the lifts broke down in the Elysium, the new shopping mall. It would be repaired within hours. Yet out here it was like visiting some far-flung, third-class world. She'd considered doing Voluntary Service Overseas after she'd left university, but she couldn't face the prospect of living where the toilets didn't flush.

She reminded herself that here too, in the first world, there was work to be done. She would bring this lift failure up at the next regional meeting. She would ask the managers why they considered that a condemned high-rise building was a suitable place to house disorientated asylum seekers, even when it was only on a temporary basis while their claim was being processed.

She dragged herself up towards the eleventh floor. At least the exercise would save her having to go to the gym that week. Since the dog's hip operation, she hadn't been able to take any decent walks along the canal.

She knew she hadn't shown enough commitment to these two. One of the difficulties was she hardly knew them. She hadn't had time to study their file. They'd been passed on to her, like a pair of nearly new shoes, when the previous WSW was redeployed to District 24. Clients there had far greater complications which could be most distressing. There were also the illegals who arrived with invented tales of political suffering in order to scrounge off the UK's medical system. Sorting them out took time. They usually ended up in the Forest Grove detention centre.

In this instance, it seemed highly probable that the two females were genuine victims. The latest terror campaign in their country of origin was being actively monitored by the Foreign Office. These investigations always took time, a delay which was doubtless an advantage for those who would eventually be deported, but hard on families trying to settle.

Level eight. Pause for breath.

Yes, she would certainly look forward to a time when she would be able to visit these two in a pleasanter part of town. She must do what she could to improve their situation. The little girl was inscrutable and seemed remarkably self-composed for her age. Could it be that living through tough times actually hardened rural people?

There was no response to a knock on the door. She was quietly relieved. It meant things were okay. The child would be in school. She had checked with the school secretary that the child had a good attendance record, so no worries there. And the woman must finally have pulled herself together and gone out to conquer her phobias.

Several residents passed, laboriously making their way up or down the stairs. She considered asking one of them about the woman and her daughter. Did they know them? Did they seem okay? However, client confidentiality was paramount, and particularly with females who had endured any kind of physical violence.

So she nodded a discreet good day to each passer-by, then she wrote a brief message and slipped it into the letterbox. She recalled that the child could speak a smattering of English. She couldn't remember if she could read yet but she would know to find someone who could. She had brought some picture books for her. They were too wide to shove through the letterbox, too thick to push under the door. She would bring them next time, when she hoped she would be able to deliver information about the new citizenship rules, and a leaflet about the toy library. The poor girl can't have enjoyed much of a childhood so far and could do with some toys.

Forgive Us Our Trespasses
as We Forgive Those

Sunday retreated to the storeroom and tried to settle the information he had received from the old lady with the South African name and the Eastern face. It would not settle. So he tried to pray.

'O merciful Lord, I have done wrong. I have lied. I am in your hands.'

After that, his mind went blank. What should he say next? In the good book it definitely stated that God would rise up and protect one against one's enemies. Yet surely it could not be correct to ask the Almighty for support in continuing on a path of deceit? So he recited that trusty faithful, the Lord's Prayer, which covered most of life's eventualities in an unspecific way.

Another Visitor for Sunday

Sunday was away from reception, attending to a gutter blocked by a pigeon's nest on the sixteenth, when a woman in a stern grey suit came looking for him. Mr McLeod was loitering in the lobby, intent on finding someone with whom to pass the time with a wee bit of a blether. The days were long. It was a sore tragedy to be healthy enough to live to seventy. He nearly died of malaria in his forties but some young laddie barely out of medical school had saved his life. He was grateful at the time. Now he wasn't so sure.

He mistook the woman for a representative from the housing office. He gave her several pieces of his mind concerning bureaucratic incompetence, poor maintenance and tardiness over the rehousing allocations.

The woman said, 'I don't have time for all that. If

you have complaints, take them to City Hall.' She left a sealed brown envelope, stamped in red with 'PRIVATE', on the caretaker's desk. When she had gone, Mr McLeod slipped the letter into his own pocket to take up to Mrs Ndebele. One positive outcome of the young lad's secret troubles was that it gave Mr McLeod a sense of purposefulness in his loitering. It was Mrs Ndebele's idea that the residents should keep an eye on the young lad.

Mrs Ndebele often blethered about her own past rather than wishing to hear about his, but at least she was company and she sometimes offered him some of her oriental food, always subtler than the over-spiced gbegiri he had to eat in his younger days.

When she opened her door to him, he told her straightaway, 'You'll ken as well as I that it's never guid news that arrives in the brown envelope. I am of the opinion some new trouble is brewing for the lad. You and I, we mebbe dinnae always see eye to eye on certain matters. But in the matter of natural justice, we are as one.'

Sunday Tries to Make a Decision

Lying on the mattress, it was hard to rest. Much was whirling through his mind. There had been no delivery of fuel. He had had to limit the boiler to heating tap water only. If even in the afternoon, he was shivering in the unheated storeroom, what of the residents stacked above him like the frozen packs on the shelves of Mr Hamid's freezer? He had advised his flock of the heating changes by means of a personal note into every letterbox. It would be difficult for Ms Sardini in 5-W who was newly delivered of a child. He had suggested she let the baby sleep in her own bed at night and spend the day bound closely to her body in a wrapper as mothers did in the village at home.

Ms Sardini had smiled, offered him an almond sweetmeat, but said nothing that he understood.

Sunday packed newspapers under the thin mattress.

172

It was not the cold that was eating into him. It was the doubt about his mission. He had surely been living in Fool's Paradise. He had made a grave mistake to allow himself to be delivered to this clogged island. He should have argued with the people smuggler in Rotterdam to send him to a more caring nation where children like Rosa did not have to live alone, where old people did not have to trek up many flights of stairs each day as if they were Himalayan village folk.

Moreover, he was achieving nothing here. Nor did he wish to live as a fugitive for ever. Perhaps he should move on. The republic of Iceland had established a government a thousand years ago, ahead of any other European country. There, freedom of speech was the law. More than ninety per cent of the people were Christians. The population was modest, fewer humans than sheep, just as it might have been in Palestine in Our Lord's time. The Icelanders might welcome a strong, healthy, willing incomer. They needed manpower to fish for fish and to shepherd their sheep, just as in Galilee.

When Sunday looked into his heart he heard its regular throb but no divine guidance. In his imagination, which operated separately from his heart, he saw Iceland, white and pure, a land of hope, though treeless as a desert and, obviously, very icy. In that climate, he would need more than his thin sweater, cotton jeans and a navy blue uniform. A thick padded jacket, a hat with ear covers and snow-proof boots would be essential. He had only two brown bank-notes remaining. That would never be enough to purchase suitable clothing. Also, the sea crossing was bound to be rough. By the grace of God, he had survived seven hours in the Atlantic Ocean at Latitude 60 degrees, but to flounder in the same ocean at Latitude 25 degrees was not a risk he wished to take.

If not Iceland, then perhaps Scotland? Scotland was attached by land to The Wonderland yet it was a separate country with its own laws and government. Mr McLeod was born there. He said that, contrary to the myth of their tight-fistedness, Scots were among the most generous and hospitable nations of the world.

Rosa Is Okay??????!!!!!

At school, Endeavour stars were awarded to those who achieved a clear dinner plate. Jules, the self-appointed bodyguard, forked her unwanted broccoli florets over on to Rosa's plate.

'Thank you, Jules. You are forever the kind friend,' said Rosa who'd just found out that 'the' could be used in all sorts of ways she hadn't thought of before. She quickly ate up the extra portion of vegetables before any of the dinner attendants noticed the great green heap on her plate and the empty space on Jules's. Then she whispered to Jules about Lila's dramatic departure.

Jules gasped. 'Wow, so you're all on your own? That's just incredible! You have such a fantastic life and you're so brave.'

'No,' said Rosa. 'Not brave. Is the life. Is what happen.'

'Actually, Rosa, you know perfectly well that I hardly know a single thing about what happened to you before you got to come here. You haven't told me anything useful. But something must have happened. I've sort of guessed a few things and I guessed some of it wasn't too good, right?'

Rosa shrugged. 'Is maybe.'

'Anyhow, Mum told me not to pry. So I won't ask. I say, d'you want to come over and stay with us?'

'Thank you. I am okay.'

'My mum, I know I say she's a pain. But she's also very understanding about orphans and all that stuff. Gives money to charity.'

Who was the orphan? Not Rosa. She had a mother and a granpap. She had all the people in the Hawk Rise who were like family, and all the people in that other place that was dark black and fiery red in her mind. She would never allow herself to become a bereaved child.

'Honest, you'd be no trouble. In fact, you'd be doing me a real favour. My mum makes me eat loads of this stuff. Rabbit food. Yuk.'

'The rabbit food nice for the rabbit. Nice for me.'

'Anyway, don't suppose you'd like it. My mum can be a right party-pooper. Doesn't let me do anything on my own. But hey, Rosie-Posie, wasn't it just about pig's bottom when you saw her go?'

'Pig's bottom?'

'Like, you know, didn't it make you feel a bit sad? I mean, I sometimes think I'd quite like my mum to be taken away. When she's baiting me about vegetables and health and that. But not really.'

Yes, it had definitely been pig's bottom to watch Lila carried away. But she was not going to kick up a stink or dwell on the mother worries. Hadn't the WSW woman told her, You've got to lead your own life?

'Also, Jules, I have the big work with my Piet.'

'What pet's that? I thought you said you weren't allowed to keep pets in that place you live.'

'Piet. My friend. Like you my the friend. He the sad man-boy. I make him the meal.'

Jules sighed enviously. 'I never knew you had a boyfriend. Gosh, Rosa, I know you must've been through tough times but sometimes I think you have all the luck too. Life's so unfair.'

Walking back from school towards an empty flat, Rosa did feel sorrowful, but it wasn't only about being left on her own. It was also that she'd disobeyed Granpap. He'd clearly told her, 'You will take care of your dear mother,' and she'd failed. From now on, she must do better.

'Geddit, girl?' she said aloud and laughed. 'That's the ticket.'

Sunday was hunched over the reception desk reading his secret book with its print as small as ants. He looked up when Rosa came in but he did not smile.

'Good afternoon, Rosa,' he said. 'You have studied well today?'

'Yes.'

'That is good. And mother's health is improving?'

Rosa shrugged.

'Have you not visited her?'

Rosa shook her head. 'The hospital is long way.'

'In my village, family members will walk fifteen miles to visit their loved ones if they are hospitalized. They do not neglect their family obligations.'

'I am not to know the direction.'

'Please, Rosa, you should visit her soon, to bring her good cheer. I could find the location and take you there. I could remain outside while you visit. I could escort you back here so you come to no harm.'

'Maybe,' said Rosa uncertainly. 'And so maybe not. Maybe it is better I see the mum later. Not now. I wait till she walks on the legs again.'

'Is it the hospital you are afraid of?' Sunday asked.

'No!' said Rosa quickly. 'I'm never afraid.' She changed the subject. 'You listen. Today I have the little fish from the tin and the mayonnaise from the tube like the toothpaste. So you eat meal together with me?'

Sunday shook his head. 'No, I am sorry. I should not do that.'

'Hah! You think I cook bad so you do not like no more? Or hah, you think if I am not visit the mum you not visit me?'

'Rosa, while you are alone, I should not come into your home. It is not customary for a male to enter a young woman's house if he is not her brother, or father or uncle. It would be shameful for me to dishonour you in that way.'

Rosa giggled. 'I am not the young woman! I am the girl!'

Sunday said, 'I cannot change the customs I have learned. When your mother returns, I will come into your home once more.'

Rosa went up the stairs feeling perplexed. How was it that he was prepared to walk across the town to find the hospital, but not to walk up the stairs to 11-N? As Jules would say, What a crazy weirdo.

When she opened the door to 11-N she found the WSW's note on the floor.

Trusting you are both settling in OK, she read. *If Any PROBLEMS, please get in touch <u>immediately</u>!!!!!!!!*
Yours, P. Smith.

Rosa was surprised by the marks of !!!!!!!! So many. Too many. Jules had put a similar line of them, like a fence, in her school workbook. Ms Martin had said, 'A single exclamation mark, Jules, conveys the essential mood adequately. More than one is excessive and not good English.'

How was Rosa expected to learn correct English if the WSW did not use it?

P. Smith had written a telephone number on her note. 11-N had no telephone installed. Nor did Rosa consider that she needed one as she had no immediate problems. She placed P. Smith's note next to the envelope which had contained the letter from the Area Health Manager and she settled to her homework.

The Interrogators

Two men, clean-shaven, in light-coloured suits, were waiting in the entrance hall when Sunday came down from inspecting Mrs Wieczerzak's cold-water tap. He had replaced the washer before. He found that the tap was still in satisfactory working condition and realized she had reported a possible drip as an opportunity to place another of her apple and cinnamon cakes into his hands.

'Looks like you could do with a bit of feeding up,' she said.

The men downstairs wanted Sunday to accompany them. 'To straighten one or two things out concerning your status in the UK,' said one.

Sunday, fearing he was being arrested, slid the cake carefully into his pocket, right side up, in case he was held for some days and given nothing to eat.

'And to discuss your asylum claim,' added the other.

Sunday had not made any claim. This might be a trick to make him admit to other things which he had not done. He heard the Ragazzi brothers clattering down the stairs. Mr McLeod might appear at any moment. Rosa was due home from school shortly. Sunday did not wish to become a public spectacle. As Auntie Pru used to say, Family dishonour should never be hung to dry in the noonday sun.

Sunday resolved to go with the men but to say as little as possible while avoiding actual untruths for he knew the gaze of the Lord was upon him. So far, they seemed coldly courteous. They drove in an ordinary car to an office-block in the town. One of the men touched his ID card to an electronic number pad to unlock the door. They entered. The door closed and clicked automatically behind them. This would have been an ideal innovation for Hawk Rise to deter non-residents from entering the building and dumping their stuff in the stairwell.

They went in single file down a narrow corridor to a stuffy room with a small window.

A sign on the wall read 'RABIES CAN KILL'. And another, 'Thank you for NOT smoking'. What a strange nation to request citizens so politely to refrain from an activity that was already legislated against.

Sunday was told to take a seat. He gripped its sides, unsure what was going to happen next. They were wearing suits. Probably, they would not hurt him. Men in suits hired other men to do the hurting. But they might keep him locked up for a while as a warning, as the militia did back home. Nobody would know he was here. If he failed to attend Rosa's garden assembly, she might ponder on the meaning of his absence. But she would not try to search for him. Nor would it be right that she should.

He glanced to the window. There were no bars. He was fit from his responsibility over seventeen levels, yet slight from his irregular diet. He could make a dash for the window, wriggle through, run like a hot wind. But what if there were guard dogs, slobbering, as guards used in some southern countries of the African continent? There might be anything out there or nothing. If he got away, where would he hide? He who hides from the wrath of the Lord in the dens and rocks of the mountains will be found. And he was not guilty.

His single wrongdoing was to take another man's

identity, though for all he knew Piet Ali had never really existed.

He told the men, 'I am not Piet Ali.'

'Yes, we know that,' said one of them as if it wasn't important.

The men had papers on the table. Sunday tried to see what they were.

'Don't be afraid,' the other said. 'We're here to help you.'

How could Sunday believe that?

He was given a cup of milky tea with a biscuit. He was asked if he had a legal representative.

He said, 'No, sir.'

He was asked if he wanted one. His father had had a lawyer who had taken the money and left the country before the trial ended.

'You are entitled to legal aid. But you have to come clean. If you change your story, everything is more difficult. You were lucky to slip in at Felixstowe.'

'It was not that place. The port was named Lowestoft.'

One of them made a few notes.

'So you knew the name of the port of disembarkation?'

'I did not know it when I arrived. I asked an

inhabitant of the town. She told me.'

Then they asked him questions about his family, when he was born and where. At what age he started school, the names of his teachers. They asked his father's name. Sunday thought of the many times Sampson had been taken for questioning. His father's interviews had often lasted for days. He always returned bruised and cut until the time when he did not return at all.

This was not the time to weep for his father. But as the questioning continued, Sunday could not keep the memories of his father out of his mind. He felt there was a harmattan blowing so strongly from the north that a sandstorm was brewing up inside his head. He couldn't hear what the men were asking and he replied Yes or No at random.

He heard one of them saying, 'I said, would you like a glass of water?'

'No,' said Sunday, then, 'Yes, please.'

After the drink, they resumed.

'Tell us again, Sunday, how you came to be on that risky journey. You say you had to leave your home because of persecution. The Foreign Office has not notified us of that area still being unsafe. Conditions are said to have been normalizing for some time.'

Sunday knew nothing of foreign office. His education at the Mission School was perhaps deficient.

'Earlier,' the other man said as he removed his jacket, 'you mentioned how you are from Rotterdam and have, I believe, never been outside Europe?'

'No,' said Sunday, touching the apple cake in his pocket as if it were a talisman. 'This is incorrect. Rotterdam was the first time for my feet to touch the soil in the continent of Europe.'

'If what you've told us about Holland is correct, how come there's no evidence of your entry into the UK? Security is tight at all known infiltration portals.'

Sunday thought. He said, 'I wanted to go to Canada. But Iceland is good. '

'As I am sure you know, if you had intended to claim asylum here in the UK, on whatever grounds, be it as an economic migrant or a political refugee, you should have done so immediately on arrival. That would have been to your advantage.'

Sunday recalled the old woman with the dog in the port of Lowestoft who had told him to proceed to an advice centre alongside a post office but he had been too confident, too arrogant, to follow her prudent recommendation.

'How old is he?' one of them mumbled to the other.

'Because if he's a minor, he might stand a better chance, wouldn't you say?'

They both looked at Sunday, bemused, like two baboons might gaze at a koala. 'Not an indefinite leave to remain but the right to continue your education and so remain here until eighteen.'

Inside his pocket, Sunday's fingers touched nervously at the sugary crust of the apple cake and an impulsive idea came to him. He should not eat this cake himself but, when he got out of here, he must deliver it to Lila in the hospital while it was still fresh.

They were explaining how the immigration procedures operated.

'But there are frequent changes to the system, most often weighted against applicants. It would be enormously beneficial if you had proof of your date of birth. If we could confirm your age you might be eligible for certain benefits.'

'We could get the unit doc in to examine him.'

'It's not a medic he needs. It's a dental examination.'

When Sunday was very young, a dentist used to turn up in the village once a year on a bicycle, his tools in a leather bag, and with a drill he worked with a foot pedal. He would set up on a stool under the tree and wait for clients to wander over. Auntie Pru had had two rotten teeth pulled. She had prayed but not cried. Afterwards she had bled. Later, she had thanked God that they lived in times of healthcare. The mobile dentist would also, for a fee, extract hens' teeth so they would not peck their neighbours.

Sunday still had all his teeth except one which was broken off when he had been hit with a riot club. All the rest were strong and white. He had bought a toothbrush from the 8-to-late. He used it regularly.

'A doctor can't do it. They're obliged to use the scanner.'

'Scanner?'

'When you suspect they're under-age, they can't do the X-rays any more. Banned. Grave ethical reservations from the Chief Medical Officer.'

'Doesn't make sense, does it? Picking up kids like this, then chucking them out on the streets. We ought to be doing more for them than that.'

They muttered to one another, shuffled their papers and stood up. The interview appeared to be over. Sunday did not know why.

'So we will be in touch again and in the meantime, you should keep us informed of any change of address, or of any changes in your circumstances.'

Sunday was offered a lift to Hawk Rise. He declined. 'It is good that I walk,' he said.

Visiting the Sick

Outside in the fresh air, Sunday asked two women standing at a bus stop the way to the hospital.

'Well, they've moved it, haven't they?' said one to the other.

'That's right. The old General used to be bang in the centre of town. But they had to go and build a new one. Progress.'

'It's all these Poles coming over, having their babies here. The General couldn't cope.'

'They've had to recruit Polish midwives.'

'There's a load of Croatians too.'

'Why they don't hire interpreters I don't know. Wouldn't that be cheaper?'

'You'd think so, wouldn't you?'

Sunday waited patiently while the women finished their discussion and were able to give him adequate directions. He had only ever been inside a hospital once before. It had been bleak with disagreeably stained walls. The new General, now renamed on a bright notice-board outside, St James' City & County, with a clean bright entrance and shiny floors, appeared to him more like a hotel.

The receptionist located Lila's name on her computer. 'She's been in isolation. She may not be allowed visitors yet. You must speak with the ward sister when you get up there.'

Sunday passed signs directing patients to the X-ray Unit. He did not understand why the interviewers had decided against subjecting him to X-rays of his teeth but he was glad. The travelling dentist had needed no such complex equipment to identify decaying teeth. He just tapped each one with a small metal utensil.

Outside Lila's ward, he was advised to cleanse his hands with chemical gel, then the ward sister asked, 'Are you a relative?'

'No. I am her neighbour. I am bringing her a gift, if that is permitted.' Back home, patients ate only what meals their relatives brought in for them. Otherwise they went hungry. But he knew it was different here.

'Very well. She is still quite poorly. You'll be her first visitor.'

Sunday looked anxiously at the long green gown he was given to put on over his own clothes.

The young nurse said, 'Don't worry. Mycobacterium tuberculosis may be on the increase but it responds ever so quickly once they start on the new drugs. Your friend's not infectious any more. But she has a low immunity so the gown's to protect her from the bacteria you'll be carrying.'

Lila was on her own in a side ward, propped up on pillows. She had a breathing tube going into her nostrils and another tube into her arm. She did not, at first, recognize Sunday.

He approached the bed shyly. He said, 'I bring you greetings from Rosa.'

Lila smiled and said something that Sunday didn't understand. He placed the apple cake on the bedside locker. 'I wanted to give you this. It was baked by Mrs Wieczerzak this morning.'

Lila said what Sunday guessed was an expression of appreciation. They shared several further exchanges, laughing, since neither understood the other's language, until Sunday said, 'Now I must go. I will tell Rosa I have seen you and that you will be well soon. And I promise you I will keep my eye on her welfare in whatever way I can. I will visit you again and bring you some of Mr McLeod's treacle tablet. Goodbye.'

But Lila held on to his arm to prevent him leaving. She was asking for something, making a gesture of writing. So Sunday fetched a scrap of paper and a pen from the nurses' station. Lila wrote her message which she gave to Sunday. She said, 'Rosa. Okay okay? Soon soon home. A1. A1.'

Sunday understood.

He made his way back to Hawk Rise slowly with tears in his eyes though he didn't know who they were for.

Everyman's Heart Must Be in Garden

Rosa was angry. 'Hey, Piet, where you been? You the late one? You been too long time away. You forget the assembly?'

'I had to go to see some people. About another matter. About identity. But it need not concern you.'

'Huh. You have the secrets?'

'Yes. But it is no secret that, on my return, I visited Lila.'

'Who give you the permission?'

'I went on your behalf.'

'You not having the right.'

'A mother has a right for reassurance that her child is well.'

Rosa felt sulky. 'Maybe.'

Sunday handed Rosa the note from Lila. Rosa

couldn't help smiling as she read it. Then, 'You, Piet, you read this already?'

'No. You know that I do not know your language.'

'So I tell you. She gives the rule for cooking. She write how for me make the potato dumplings.' She grinned and waved the scrap of paper with its scribbled recipe at Sunday. Then she put her arms round him and gave him a quick hug. 'Piet Ali, I so sorry I had angry. You are my good A1 friend. Also Lila say here, Please no visit. She not want her Rosa there see her thin. Is same what I tell you before, huh? So now we both happy and go to assembly.'

She trotted ahead to join the people who were standing beside the burned-out van. There were nine of them. Rosa was disappointed. She wanted more, at least one representative from every flat. 'Some lazy sheeps there are,' she muttered. 'Not keen as the mustard. Not lift the finger.' She'd hoped that Enzo's brother who'd helped shift some of the rubbish might come.

The small group of adults were solemn. They were expressing opinions which Rosa found baffling. They did not seem to be talking about gardens or rubbish.

'It is indeed high time we took action,' said Mr Hamid.

Rosa wondered why he was there when he did not live in the Hawk Rise tower.

Mr Hamid went on, 'I too am affected by this prospect of imminent upheaval. As some of you may know, the lease on my store is not to be renewed. They are adamant on this.'

Mr Aziz, from 16-S, nodded. 'We should form a committee. Nobody in authority will bother to listen if we don't approach them with a democratically elected working group.'

Mrs Wieczerzak said, 'They won't pay attention anyway, whatever we say. To them, we are nothing but small small people. They think we are not worthy of their bother.'

Mr Hamid said, 'I greatly regret I cannot stay longer to debate this as I have left Mrs Hamid in charge and she is not confident with the till. But please keep me informed. I wish to be involved.'

Rosa plucked at Sunday's sleeve. 'What is happen?' she hissed. 'They not up to the scratch?'

Sunday said quietly, 'Our neighbours are assembled to discuss a different serious matter.'

'Garden matter is serious.'

'They are expressing concern for the future of the building.'

Mrs Stuart, 6-W, said, 'What's the point in a committee? Everybody knows they're to close the place whatever. It's been on their agenda for yonks.'

'Yonks?' said Rosa. 'What is?' Nobody was listening to her.

'And us?' asked Mr Swaniji. 'What will become of us?'

Mr Johnson said, 'So long as you're properly British, not half and half, you'll be right as rain, though it's tough on pensioners. Some have lived here since forever.'

Mrs Wieczerzak put up her hand. 'Yes, I am one of your antiques. I moved in the same week as Mrs Ndebele. I still have my first rent book. But it is not us with full citizenship who are the worry. It will be unsettling but not the end of the world. At least they will deposit us in some sunset home. It's poor souls like the Florians and the Mohammeds, the Dioufs and the Osmans we must consider. What security have they?'

There were murmurs of agreement.

'Take Mr Diouf. He's been waiting to hear from the Home Office for months. There's only so many times they can appeal.'

'Aye, she is hitting the nail right on the heid,' said

Mr McLeod with vigorous head-nodding. 'It's a gleg manner to be rid o' all the ones they cannae be fashed to deal with. Some of the clandestines have nae place to go. So it will be back into detention. Then it's only a wee step to deportation. And that would be a humiliation on all oor heids.'

'No, Mr McLeod,' said Mrs Wieczerzak. 'Surely, they won't deport anybody. Specially not any of the young ones. They'd never send them back on their own to Lord knows what. Dispersal is their current policy, to other areas.'

'Spread them thin so they don't have a collective voice,' agreed Mrs Ndebele. 'Those three young lads up on seventeen, they'll have them separated off before you can say knife.'

'Aye, first the dispersal. Then the extradition. Like the merciless malice o' of the Highland Clearances. Two hundred years on and it is nae different. The powerful crush the weak and the poor.'

'It's still only rumour,' said Mrs Stuart. 'First I heard was last week.'

'Then you bide with your heid in the sand.'

The adults argued. Rosa listened. What had happened to her important garden meeting? 'Yonks yonks,' she grumbled and stomped off to attack a new drift of rubbish which had been dumped by the fence.

Sunday joined her. His shoulders drooped like a wet cat in a deep pond.

'Why?' she demanded. 'Why are these yonks?'

'There has been a confusion of intent. They misinterpreted the meaning of the poster. The people who built the Tower of Babel to the glory of Jehovah suffered similarly. When all the people of the world speak with the single voice of love, there will be no more problems.'

'Is quite out of order.'

'Failure of correct communication can happen when passions are hot.'

'And what we do now, tick-tack, sprightly as the rat?'

'We find our inner strength through our trust in the power of the Lord.'

'And Bob's your uncle, we make them to the rubbish helping?'

'Rosa, have you not listened? There is a greater problem ahead than creating a garden. That is the matter under discussion, what is to become of the people.'

'So what they do? Do talk talk talk. Ms Martin she say, Less talk talk, please children, more work work.'

'Many great figures have had to fight against adversity.'

'I do not fight. My family, we like the life. We not kill the others. To fight is bad. My granpap say.'

Sunday said, 'Not with fists. People fight with their hearts. They persevere with what they believe is right. How many times did Moses go to Pharaoh's palace? How often did he have to plead before he was free to lead his people to the promised land? There must be a promised land for these people.'

'I not know the yonks. I not know the moses. I not know the promised land. Many things I not know. I know the potato dumplings. One day I know everythings.'

Sunday said, 'Moses was a great prophet. Another time I will explain.'

'Yonks prophet adversity!' Rosa giggled. 'Sometimes you so serious, Piet. And sometimes you the funny man, say funny things. But you always my nice friend.'

'Rosa, listen. There is something further I have to tell you. I am not good. I have done some bad things.'

'You kill the other man? That much bad?'

'No, not like that.'

'Then is okay.'

'I have lied to you. My name is not Piet.'

Rosa shrugged. 'So no Piet. Same like my granpap, he never say, Rosa. Always he say, Angel. What other name you have?'

'Sunday.'

'Very nice good okay-dokay name. I like this. And now you my Sunday friend and we do the garden rubbish.'

Sunday shook his head. 'No, Rosa. It is not worth the effort. Don't you understand? The building is going to be demolished.'

She wrinkled her nose as if she had no idea what he meant. So he gathered up a handful of rubbish and threw it up in the air. 'Like that. Goodbye Hawk Rise.'

She laughed. She understood but did not believe him. 'You still funny friend.'

Sunday had promised Lila that he would watch over Rosa. How was he to do that when his own situation was just as precarious? He said, 'Rosa, I have under the desk in the hall some sag aloo gifted from Mrs Khan. Would you like to share?'

'No way. Sag aloo too spicy stinky,' said Rosa. 'I live own life. I cook potato dumplings. You want share, you come up.' She ran into the building and made for the stairs.

Sunday watched her go. Rosa was so vulnerable. She believed she was invincible. Perhaps there was, after all, more of the Lord's work for him to do.

Prudence's Predicament

Prudence reflected how, in these days of decreasing faith, Old Testament tales were seen to be useful parables rather than historical events. Even the parting of the Red Sea, which had enabled Moses to lead his people to freedom, was now considered to be no divine work but a natural relocation of water following a violent earthquake. Yet who was it, if not God, who decreed when the earthquakes and tsunamis should occur? There must, surely, be a plan behind the chaos and catastrophes? So what was God's plan for Sunday?

The camp was an enclosed world where stale rumours continued to flourish as fast as the cockroaches under the tent flaps. Two survivors from the pirogue disaster, it was now being said, had been adopted by a charitable organization and were being despatched to families in

Canada. Was one of those boys Sunday? Meanwhile, three other survivors, so the story went, had swum all the way to the North African coast, had begun planning another attempt to reach Europe, only to be arrested by Moroccan coastguards.

Was Sunday among that group? If so, would he be repatriated? And where to? To the vastness of tentland? To the village? To some foreign village? To an internment camp? Would he have any choice?

Prudence, at least, still had free will to make her own decisions about her fate. Whether or not Sunday were alive, she must return to the village. She had seen how people died here in anonymity. Every hour of every day, a dozen or more were placed in the communal grave to be scattered with lime. Her death, an event which was surely imminent, would be just one more statistic without mourners.

She wanted the moment when she encountered her Lord to happen beneath a familiar sky with the tall mountain clouds around, among the memory of familiar smiles. She wanted her remains to lie in the same red earth from which she had come.

However, by leaving, might she be hastening her death? To die by one's own action was an offence against the giver of life. And then, suppose, through

His munificent grace, He enabled her to reach the village safely, what would she do for water?

The old borehole, four miles distant, had been damaged during the insurgence. The small well nearby had always been green with algae and was used also by passing animals whose droppings contaminated the supply.

When she had been a child, the well-water was always boiled before use. Then, the wood supplies dwindled and this use of fuel was too wasteful. They drank the water and took the risks. If you didn't get sick, you got the parasites. There was not a child in the village who had not been wriggling inside with worms and flukes. Yet that too was life, part of God's magnificent yet mysterious plan.

Making Light of Rosa's Labour

There were no offers of help as she went on with clearing the ground. Enzo appeared and sat silently near her dangling his piece of string. It was odd him saying so little. Maybe it was because his brothers were so loud.

Martino came down too, but only to shout and kick a tin can about.

Rosa said, 'Why your big brother do not come help lending me a hands?'

Martino shrugged. 'Pacco doesn't have time to play. Got a lot of serious responsibility.'

'This is serious responsibility. Not play. I am the strong ox.'

Martino just laughed and wandered off. 'Suit yourself,' he said.

Rosa muttered, 'Your brother, weedy. You too.'

One of the bully-girls at school had called her weedy. It did not refer to the fact, as Rosa had thought, that she was prepared to eat somebody else's unwanted green vegetables and could be knocked over by a flying crayon, but that she had thin legs.

Some of the grown-up people occasionally paused to observe Rosa at work.

'You're a braw young lassie,' said Mr McLeod. 'But I hae ma doots if yon ground will ever be broken. It is solid as pure granite.'

'When will you start your double-digging?' called Mr Brown, the ambulance caller from floor twelve, with a cheery wave as he went off to work.

'No hoaxing. No jokey. This is the serious responsibility,' said Rosa. 'To make the beautiful garden. When is my harvest time, then you not laugh.'

'That's right, my dear,' said Mrs Wieczerzak. 'Having a play garden is a lovely little project for you,' and she patted Rosa on the head.

'I not hound dog!'

'Try not to take offence so quickly. You've a dear little face. A pretty smile doesn't cost much, does it?'

Rosa knew she would smile and be happy once the garden greened. Where passers-by could see only piles of refuse and small patches of sour dust, Rosa willed herself to see sunflower faces turning through the day, straight rows of maize growing taller than Granpap, their silky tassels waving in the breeze, their leaves rustling as they dried. She could see the cobs ripen to gold. She saw herself pluck them. Some to eat, some to feed to her hens, their feathers tawny, ochre or russetty brown as they pecked between the vegetables, keeping the earth free of weeds.

Hens, when kept in close confinement through the winter months, bullied and pecked at one another. Not Rosa's. Her committee of fowl would learn amicability and mutual respect.

Rosa saw herself throwing out the kernels of corn to her flock before collecting up their eggs in an apron. She smiled. Granpap would be pleased. When the hens were reality, she could borrow Jules's mother's camera and get a picture to send.

Prudence Dreams

There were two dreams, each a retelling of a story she already knew, one from the Old Testament, one from the New. The first was of Moses who had not remained in one place but was constantly on the move, from infancy when he floated down the Nile in a basket until extreme age when he led his people on their exodus out of Egypt.

The other dream was of Joseph and Mary, mother of God, who yearned for the quiet, industrious life of craftspeople but were constantly obliged to travel.

Through these tales, God was telling Prudence that journeying was part of the committed life.

Each day greater numbers of refugees arrived at the camp than departed. Mostly they came on foot. The heavily laden trucks which arrived were delivering rations to the feeding stations, and teams of fresh aid workers who believed they could change the pain of the world by their good deeds, to take the place of the disillusioned and exhausted.

There would surely be a space for Prudence on one of the near-empty departing trucks. This would take her part of the way. After that, she would walk.

In childhood, she had walked seven miles to school and the same back. As a young woman she had walked further than seven to work. She was no longer young but she was determined. She could probably manage twenty a day, if she was not sick or injured. Perhaps even twenty-five.

When a person wishes to travel fast, they travel alone. But when a person wishes to travel far, they travel in a group. So she waited till she had identified others who were also planning to leave.

They filled water bottles and set out across the camp for the truck park.

'Bless our journey, O Lord,' Prudence said.

'Inshallah. If Allah wishes it,' came the quiet response from an old man so thin he seemed to be made from dry sticks.

A Public Tip

From his desk he could see Rosa working as industriously as an ant and it worried him greatly for in the book resting on his lap, he had just read, 'To every thing there is a season, and a time to every purpose under the heaven. A time to be born, and a time to die. A time to plant, and a time to pluck up that which is planted.' Now was no time for her to be planting.

When she had finished for the evening, she came in, giving Sunday a dark scowl as she passed. After she had gone up to 11-N, Sunday went out to inspect what she had been doing. He saw she had cleared a small patch of ground which she had surrounded with a protective barrier of debris. In the rectangle of feeble soil, she had set two short drills of seed. She had pierced the paper packet on to a rusty spike and stuck it at the head of one of the drills. The colourful picture indicated that she had planted radishes. Mr Hamid must have given them to her, offering her false hope, encouraging her in a project for which there could be no future.

The following day, Sunday noticed how rubbish had begun to appear beside the burned-out van. He feared that the residents, in clearing their flats prior to moving out, had taken up fly-tipping just like everybody else. He was mistaken. The cracked coal scuttle, blue plastic child's sand spade, bent rake, broken bench, aluminium bin and other items outside the van were all intended as useful contributions for Rosa's plot. She had taken over the burned-out van as her shed and sat in there to do her homework before her manual work.

Beside her plot stood a metal bin, a former container for molasses. It had become the composting receptacle and soon began to fill with used tea bags, cabbage stalks, potato parings, apple cores, deposited by residents.

Sunday observed Mrs Ndebele shuffle out with a vacuum-cleaner dust bag which she shook out into the bin.

Rosa was gently combing her plantation with a bent fork to rid it of non-existent weeds. The likelihood of anything germinating in that poor soil seemed slight.

Sunday watched Rosa strut over to Mrs Ndebele.

'What you do now?' she asked. 'Who give you the permission? This my garden.'

Mrs Ndebele laughed. 'There's nothing I don't know about mixing a good compost, precious petal, but in my day we called it home fertilizer. When you been born next to a swamp, you use up every last thing you got. No corporation refuse collection back then. You know what, we used even our night-soil to nourish that ground!'

'Night-soil?' Rosa was puzzled.

Mrs Ndebele explained in a simple mime what she meant.

'Huh! That most very stinky.'

Mrs Ndebele shrugged. 'Fine stink of fruitfulness. But you mustn't go doing it in these days. There's laws against it, I dare say. Well, better be getting along now, buttercup.'

To Sunday, she said as she returned, 'Isn't it a fine thing to see the child enjoy a little bit of earthly paradise?'

Sunday nodded politely, though he could not agree. Only those with a misguided imagination could see Rosa's patch resembling any kind of paradise. It was more like a nightmare waiting to happen. What would she do when she learned that this whole site, her garden included, was soon to be destroyed?

Ten Green Fingers

Two plants, already bearing healthy green leafage, were brought to the burned-out van. The first one was a gift from Martino.

'It's a conker.' It was sprouting in a used pesto jar of water. 'A winning champion last autumn. I been keeping it ever since. But Pacco told me I got to get rid of it before we move out. He says it's like me. More trouble than it's worth. But I think he loves me. And I love my conker. It's going to grow up into the most mighty conker tree you ever seen. You take good care of him, heh?'

Rosa had no idea what a conker tree might look like. Or what useful harvest it might produce. But she helped Martino plant it in a position of his choice.

He said, 'Listen, I'm sorry about the other day. But I've got a lot on my mind. We all have. Specially Pacco.

Enzo's quite a handful.'

'What about your mum? Why she not care?'

He shook his head. 'No mum.' He drew his fingers across his throat.

'Dead?'

Martino nodded.

'So father dad? He also is . . . ?' Rosa drew her fingers across her throat as Martino had done.

'No. But he got took away.'

'Policemen?'

''Course not. He's not a thief or nothing. Just bad papers.'

'So why you not took away also?'

'Pacco heard them coming. Hid us under the sink, didn't he?'

Rosa felt so sad she was almost sick. She wanted to hug Martino. But she knew that would upset him much more.

After Martino's conker, Mr Emanuel Jackson brought down an avocado, one metre tall with five broad leaves. 'I been growing him in ma bathroom from the stone since last year. It's time he took a taste of the sunlight and the fresh air before it's too late and this place go boom. His name is Joey.'

'And what fruit?' Rosa asked.

'Oh no, honey, there ain't no chance in hell of this little chap growing no fruit. Too chilly in this damn place. And maybe he won't even get through another British winter. But you know why I love him so? You want to guess?'

Rosa guessed. 'Maybe you have no friend, so that why you love the plant?'

'No. I love him because he reminds me of ma grandma. She has an avocado in her yard.'

Mr Jackson suggested a spot close, but not too close, to the conker. 'So they keep one another company after we all gone away! But not crowd each other either.'

He dug a hole with the blue plastic sand spade and, on the insistence of Rosa, dropped in a spadeful of mixture from the compost bin even though it had not yet begun to decompose. And so the little tree was planted.

Rosa was delighted. The two spindly saplings gave the plot, surrounded by its curious shield of refuse, the appearance of being finally under cultivation.

' "Butter of the poor" they call them back home,' Mr Jackson explained. 'When them fruit start ripening, all the starving skinnyrat kids start fattening like pigs. They come sneaking through the picket fence, help themselves to Grandma Meredith's fruit. Eat till they are bursting. Grandma keeps a close watch on that tree.'

When the first green leaves of the radishes began to show as imperceptible green lines Rosa was so excited that she could not resist telling Jules.

Jules was impressed by everything Rosa told her. 'Wow. It's just like that story of *The Secret Garden*, you know, the lonely waif who comes from far-off Eastern lands where everybody's died and then she turns out to have green fingers.'

'No green fingers,' said Rosa, showing them. 'All very clean. And no secret. This is share for all the peoples of my home.'

'And does your boyfriend help, with the digging and heavy stuff?'

'Boyfriend?'

'Wednesday. Or whatever you said he's calling himself now. Or was it Friday? Like Man Friday in *Robinson Crusoe*? Your own servant. Wow fantastic. I always said you get all the luck.'

'Him? He not the boyfriend. He not help. He big no-bother pain in back,' said Rosa firmly.

Sign Here Please

Jules asked every morning, 'You okay then?'

'Cool. I do good soup. No worries.'

And this was quite true. Rosa's life had become easier to manage now that Lila wasn't here in the flat. Sunday had said Lila was safe and Rosa knew he wouldn't lie about a thing like that.

Because she wasn't worried about Lila, because she didn't have to keep getting up in the night for her, Rosa slept better and hardly had any bad dreams at all.

After school, Rosa took her vouchers down to the 8-to-late to exchange for her supper. She ate her supper. She washed her socks and her briefs with the remains of the bar of slimy soap which was now down to a thin sliver. She considered asking Mr Hamid if he was allowed to give her soap for a voucher rather than food.

But decided not to bother since socks washed perfectly well in cold water.

She said goodnight to Granpap's blurry face. She put herself to bed. She woke and got back to school in time for the canteen breakfast.

Nobody had ever seen Lila escort Rosa to school, or seen Lila waiting at the gate at home time, so nobody missed her. Rosa appeared clean and tidy. Her hair was braided. No nits.

Jules's mother tried to speak to her. 'Are you sure everything's all right, Rosa?' she asked.

Rosa knew that Jules must have broken her promise not to tell. What friendship was that?

'Okay, thank you. Very okay.'

'Who's taking care of you?'

'Many loadsa friends. Garden friends.'

'Garden friends?' said Jules's mother.

'All taking nice care. Mr Brown. He has the mobile and give me the radish. Mrs Wieczerzak, a bit old. Not as old as Mrs Ndebele. All the many peoples.'

Jules's mother said, 'But surely there should be some official adult as well?'

'Is okay. Home Office know we wait the appeal now. Not long to go.'

'Isn't there a social worker or some appropriate carer?'

'Yes. Is okay. WSW. Pauline. Very good. I'm good, and very nice, thank you.'

It went on being okay nice until Rosa needed the signature of authorization from parent or guardian for the class outing. They were to travel by coach to an art gallery, then to a museum about industry, finally to see the Angel of the North. In design and technology, they'd all nearly finished their scale models which stood on the shelves around the classroom keeping guard with their outstretched wings over their other lessons.

Everybody was going on the trip. Rosa was excited. She took her form to Sunday. She would not let his annoying behaviour get in the way of this chance of going on the trip.

'I am so cross to you before,' she said. 'Now I am very sorry for that. And I need you write your name. Please if you please. Here, on dotty line. Just the name.'

He shook his head. 'I am sorry, Rosa.'

She was astonished. 'What you sorry! What you not do this for me?' She tried pleading. 'Please, Sunday. Is no hoax. Just the name.'

'I cannot do this for you.'

'Your name too special, huh? No lie. No pretend you are parent. You just do it, do it, do it.' That was what the teacher said to Jules when she refused to get on with her work.

'Sincerely, Rosa, I cannot comply with this. I have explained it before. My signature would be invalid. I have no identity here. It would bring no benefit to you. It is better you ask Mr McLeod, or Mr Hamid. They have a good writing style and are of great maturity.'

Rosa was furious. 'You no more the nice friend! The number one, you no like my garden, you no be bother. All the other folk bother and help. Also the number two, now you no help me again with visit the north angel man. You the traitor.'

Sad Sunday

He would not let himself become involved with Rosa's garden until after dark. Then he crept out to dribble water gently along the seed drills while a half-remembered mission hymn about ploughing and scattering on God's good land hummed through his head. He fetched a second bucketful to pour more liberally over the two sapling trees.

He had heard about the origins of the little avocado, how Mr Jackson had been germinating it on the windowsill of 10-S to keep in mind his grandmother's avocado in her Jamaican yard.

How many lonely souls around the world kept a beloved sitting in their hearts in the shade of a special tree? If only he could have shared his memories with Mr Jackson. But it was not his role to burden others with his sorrows at a time when they had troubles enough of their own. He must rejoice in what he had. Hawk Rise was still the blessed tree which gave him shade and shelter. And the fruits of this tree, despite their irregularities and odd behaviours, were a harvest of which to be proud.

The most vulnerable of all the fruits was Rosa whom he had failed so dismally. In what way could he ever make amends?

Mrs Ndebele's Mango and Sago Dessert

Rosa didn't want to take Sunday's advice and ask Mr McLeod for the signature. She could never understand him properly. Nor did she want to ask Mr Hamid, even though he was friendly, enquiring every afternoon, 'How is your mother? It is a while since we have seen her.'

Rosa replied, 'Thank you, my mother is fine, thank you.'

She went up to 14-E. She could hear the television. She tapped on the door. She called through the letterbox. 'In need bit of the help!'

There was no reply so she sat down to wait, remembering what Granpap used to tell her about showing respect to old people because, if you are fortunate, one day you too will be old.

With her book on her knees, she started on her homework. It was exciting doing Creative Writing because you could write any way you felt and Ms Martin didn't make a fuss about spelling and punctuation. She'd asked pupils to write what the Angel of the North might see from his high vantage point. It was supposed to be written after the class trip rather than before. But Rosa already knew from behind her own eyes what he could see. So she described the fluffy-topped carrots growing round his huge metal feet, the orchard of almond trees blossoming beyond, the prairie of rustling maize, and way on the distant horizon the oasis with its fruit-laden date-palms. It was a bountiful mixture of what she could remember of the valley at home and of what she imagined Sunday's village might be like.

She was about to add what the Angel of the North was thinking when the door of 14-E opened.

'Did I hear the noise of a little gecko? Ah, it's Gaia, our garden girl! Were you waiting for me, petal?'

Rosa nodded. 'To ask the special nice kind thing, no hoax.'

'As I've told you before, you shouldn't sit on that cold step, flower.'

Rosa got up.

'And no school today then? I thought you liked it?'

'Done school. Finish two o'clock. Teacher Inset day.'

'Teacher insect? Whatever will they think of next?'

'Special teacher day. Refresh minds. Then day after class outing. So I got in big fix.'

'What big fix, lovey? What's happened? They been calling you names? If it's bad names, you have to stand up to them.'

'Not bad names,' said Rosa. She was no longer a target. Instead, a more recent newcomer was having to put up with the bullies. Then, after a while, there'd be an even newer new person and the bullies could start all over again.

'Whatever it is, you tell me all about it. Share your little troubles, that's the way. However bad it's been, you won't be able to tell me anything I haven't experienced already. Wars, fires, typhoons, deaths and disasters. As for the late Mr Ndebele, he was the worst of it. But you haven't had to face a sour marriage yet, have you, sweetheart? So did I tell you about my Billy? Now he was my only true love.'

Mrs Ndebele's mind was like a happy hen, pecking wherever it fancied. This happened, Rosa knew, as a person grew old. Sometimes, you had to shoo their memories back in the direction you wanted them. She explained about needing a signature for the school trip.

'You really want to go, do you? Quite right too. Can't have Cinderella left behind.'

Rosa held out the permission form for Mrs Ndebele to see.

Mrs Ndebele squinted at it. 'So the reading and writing is maybe hard for your ma? Not to worry. No need for all the people in the world to read and write. You're a good girl, helping her.'

Mrs Ndebele had got it wrong. Lila was not an illiterate. Of course she could write and read, just not in the English way. After Jules had betrayed her, Rosa hadn't meant to tell anyone else how she was living alone. But now, in order to defend her mother's reputation, she let it out.

Mrs Ndebele waggled her head from side to side. 'Ah. Aha. Ah, ah, ah, Ayee. Now here maybe *is* a knotty fix to solve.'

'Please not tell. My friend say, If Ms Martin know I got to put in the Karl Wood.'

'The Carwood?'

'Yes. It is for the locker-up.'

'The locker-up?'

'Locked-up, locked-in, with the bars. In the prison for the foreigners who must go.'

'Those immigration people, they're a peculiar bunch. Should've locked up my Mr Ndebele. Never did. But not prison for you, ducky pet. You're only a little girl. They don't put children in prison here.'

'Or my Lila put to the prison? After the hospital? Then I am put to caring, my friend Jules say, to live with the strangers who are not knowing me.'

'Foster care? Well, it might not be so bad. Listen, petal-flower, you better step in. We'll have a taste of something delicious to lighten our troubles.'

Rosa followed Mrs Ndebele into 14-E.

Rosa hadn't been inside any of the flats other than 11-N. Mrs Ndebele's was the same shape, yet so different. The air smelled thick, of something which wasn't soap and wasn't perfume. The walls were dark red and deep pink. And it was crowded with possessions. Rugs on the floor, painted hangings on the walls, silk orchids in tall glass vases, carved stools, bamboo shelves and enough china ornaments of dogs and little men to start a market stall. How had she managed to hold on to so many items for so many years?

The television, with a screen as wide as one of the windows, was on at high volume.

'My rujak was no success. I tried it with the old Scot. Surly type. Didn't fancy it. They eat nothing but dried oats where he comes from. So I did a mango and sago. Do you like dessert?'

At school, dessert was brightly coloured custard sauce poured over a soft cake called sponge.

'Sago isn't to everybody's taste. I like to use palm sugar. Mr Hamid can't supply this. So it had to be British sugar. They make it from roots. Whoever wants sugar made from beet roots? Cane sugar would be better than that. But palm is always the best.'

There was another television in the kitchen recess. This was tuned to a different programme. Why two televisions? Was she lonely? When Rosa was lonely down on level eleven, she slept. Television was no cure for the loneliness when it so often showed real-life news disasters or false stories of wealthy young men and women.

Mrs Ndebele darted this way and that, searching.

'My pen is here,' Rosa offered.

But Mrs Ndebele was looking for an oven cloth. She moved Rosa out of the way so she could reach the stove where a bamboo cage was balanced over a pan of steaming water. Mrs Ndebele's knobbly hands were trembling as she lifted the cage out of the billowing steam.

'Is maybe dangerous?' Rosa said, offering to help.

But the old woman didn't want any help. Rosa had to stand back and watch as she slowly as a snail spooned grey snowballs out of their bamboo cooking baskets.

'You know what, ducky? I been watching you with your bit of planting down there. And the nice young man. Reminds me of when I was young. In our village we grew all the fruits of paradise. Pineapple, pomegranate, starfruit, longan and mangosteen. Custard apple, you ever tried that one?'

Rosa needed the signature more than she needed to talk about fruit. She could easily counterfeit Lila's signature. But this might risk Lila's place in the safe hospital bed. She held out the form.

'If you would please so kind?' She mustn't seem to be pleading. She'd seen her mother plead, right down in the dirt on her knees. It was humiliating. 'I have the pen here. Because you are the kindheart, I am thinking for you this is just the job.'

'In a moment, flower-petal, everything in its proper time, as the good Lord told us. Right now it's time for you to have a bit of feeding up. You're little more than a scrap of girl. Dumplings first, sago after. There's more than enough for two.'

If Rosa wanted a wobbly signature from those shaky hands, she had to remain as patient as a hunting cat.

The Go-between

Sunday designated himself Lila's official visitor. He made his way across town to the St. James' City & County, to take her two lamb dolmades wrapped in tinfoil, an offering he had received from Mrs Papaconstantinou. He returned with another handwritten recipe which Lila wanted him to give to Rosa.

He decided he must buy her a notebook and a stick of paste from Mr Hamid's 8-to-late so that Rosa could keep the recipes safely. But there was more to be done in order to redeem himself.

Very soon, Rosa was going to require a suitable place to live until her mother was discharged from the hospital. Sunday knew the uncertainty of being without a parent or a home. Mercifully for him, his Auntie Pru had come forward. Rosa had no perceptible aunts.

Sunday cast around for suitable alternatives but there was nobody here. Many of the residents were single males, or were far too old to cope with a girl of such vigour. He thought of Ms Sardini in 5-W but she was exhausted by her new baby whose cries could be heard all night long. Sunday prayed earnestly for the image of a suitable aunt figure to come to him.

Mrs Ndebele and the Five-spice Dumplings

She served them on an oval dish, patterned with blue dragons with golden fiery tongues. These were unlike any dumplings that Lila or Lila's mother had ever made.

'They're the five-spice Chao-Mi. When I was a kiddie, we thought they were extra extra. We had them in the dragon boat festival. My daddy used to buy them for us from the hawker stall. Either these or the Zhao Cheng.'

Mrs Ndebele handed Rosa a pair of chopsticks. Rosa clasped one in each hand. She did not know how to approach the grey dumpling.

'No, ducky, never like that. Hold both in the same hand, like scissors. You never done this before?'

Rosa shook her head.

'My Billy, he had an open outlook. He took to them straightaway. But Mr Ndebele, that rogue, he wouldn't be bothered. Told me it was uncivilized. What did he know about civilization? But he was barely down from the trees himself.'

Rosa struggled with the chopsticks.

'You can use a fork if you like, sweetie. Don't need to finish them if you don't care for them.'

'Yes, I like very nearly much already. My granpap tell me I learn to like everything.'

The comfort of eating, even if the food was unfamiliar, gave Rosa confidence. She spoke about Granpap's cow and about another type of dumplings. Then she hesitated. How much more could she share? Could she tell Mrs Ndebele about the unpleasant things? How she had sat beside Lila through interviews with the officials with their suits and their brown files in their stuffy rooms with no pictures on the walls? And how she'd had to explain to these strangers events which she herself hardly understood?

She had trusted Mrs Ndebele with part of the information, about Lila. Perhaps she should reveal the rest? 'We have the no-no good papers,' she began. 'Some good ID. Not all the papers. Some papers okay. Some, my granpap buy some. So the prison is maybe, yes. I had the friend in the Fairview. Older friend. Now I think she is in the lock-up. So maybe the school trip to see the Angel Man of the North is only last chance before my lock-up.'

She described the peaceful English home she had expected, with red tiles on the roof, standing in its garden with the coloured gnome fishing in an ornamental pool, but how that had only been a dream of her own, and even 11-N Hawk Rise was only a temporary stop-off before a move to somewhere else. 'This is all the secret. I am spilling the bean but you are not tell others.'

'My dear petkins! We all know about these things. It's not just you and the lad downstairs. There's more than half the folk in this block waiting for news from Lunar House. Take those three lads on the top floor. The big one, he can't be more than fourteen if he's a day, but he's been managing the other two somehow since the father was taken.'

Rosa nodded. 'Yes. I know this.'

'I offered help but he's too proud.'

'Taken,' said Rosa. 'Where to taken?'

'Don't you fret about it, petkins. He'll be back. As for us old wrinklies, we're waiting too, for the keys to the golden gates. Though there'll be discrimination there, I dare say. Saint Peter's a fussy fellow. Don't know who he'll be letting in.'

Rosa spent the night on the couch in 14-E as Mrs Ndebele said that it wasn't right for Rosa to be alone and Rosa decided it wasn't safe for such a confused old woman with shaky hands to be left on her own, specially when the stairwell outside was so dark.

'And the signature?' Rosa asked, as Mrs Ndebele tucked a red satin quilt round her.

'Plenty of time for that in the morning, ducky pet. And another task for tomorrow, to fetch your things here. If there's questions asked, I can say you're my granddaughter.'

Rosa didn't want Mrs Ndebele for a grandmother. She wanted her for her signature. She said sleepily, 'That is the untruth. The grandmamma's dumplings are not the same as the five-spice of you.'

'Very well, sweetheart. I'll see what I can do to improve the situation.'

Gossip on the Stairs

The first people were beginning to be moved out, rehoused in areas which had not been scheduled for commercial redevelopment. Older people were being sent to residential care. Mrs Wieczerzak and Mr McLeod met for an exchange of information. Mrs Wieczerzak had received notification that she had been allocated a place in Silverlawns Eventide Home.

'A Christian organization,' she said with a smile. 'Of all the places I should end up. 'Just so long as they don't try to make me join in their hymns of praise.'

Mr McLeod had received a similar letter advising him of a shared room at Sunnysides.

'Sunnysides and Silverlawns,' he spluttered. 'What glaikit manner o' names are these?'

'Well, at any rate, we'll be only two streets apart so we can keep in touch,' said Mrs Wieczerzak.

'If I have a mind to,' grumbled Mr McLeod.

'And I believe Mrs Ndebele has had her letter too. But she hasn't accepted yet. They're not allowing people to bring cats or dogs or cage-birds into her place.'

'What are you blethering on about? That'll nae bother Mrs Ndebele. She has never kept a cat. Her people like goldfish for good luck. Never a cat, nor a dog.'

'It's the little girl we've all been fretting about. Didn't you know? Mrs Ndebele's taken a real shine to her. I believe she wants to take her in, look after her. Just like she tried to take care of the three motherless boys. And they wouldn't have it.'

Mr McLeod had not known. 'Och fegs!' he said. 'She's a fine woman but that wee lassie, she's in need o' some taming. The two o' them together, that will make for a right tapsalteerie.'

Securing the Signature

Rosa dreamed of her wrinkle-faced, knobble-fingered Granpap. To wake in the morning on level fourteen facing east, and remember he wasn't in this country, made her sad. No dreaming was always best for then there was less to be upset about.

Then she remembered there was still the problem of the signature. She half fell off the couch and scrambled herself into her school clothes, with unwashed socks and briefs. She hated wearing yesterday's socks.

Mrs Ndebele was shuffling about in a red satin housecoat. Thank goodness she hadn't died in the night, though she looked frail enough to crumble into dust, then Rosa would never go anywhere except to the detention centre.

Mrs Ndebele was busy with a complicated tea preparation and wouldn't be fussed. 'In a while, precious. I'm busy thinking what I shall cook for our supper tonight. There's too much rush rush rush in the world today. What's the point when we're all going to end up as dust?'

The special tea had a harsh taste. It had taken so long to infuse and strain that Rosa was afraid she'd be late for school and lose one of the Endeavour stars she'd worked for so hard.

She gulped down the nasty tea, held the permissions form in front of Mrs Ndebele and showed where the signature must go.

'I can see, ducky pet. I'm not quite blind. But I have to read it first. Never sign anything you don't understand. My daddy told me that. Good advice. Remember it.'

Rosa waited.

'Very well, petal. The museum of the industrial revolution and the Angel of the North. Those should be interesting. I shall strike out where it says parent or guardian. I shall write neighbour. Then there'll be no deceit. Such things can easily rebound.'

Rosa said, 'Mrs Ndebele, I go for the school now.'

But Mrs Ndebele had stumbled into another memory store. It was impolite to interrupt old people. 'So of course it was easy for me, with Billy a squaddie in the British army. They understood in those days. Lots of the lads married local girls. It was just a shame he went so soon. And there were no babies. My sisters all had so many. Too many, my aunt said. But if you don't have babies, you don't get the grandchildren.'

At last she handed back the completed form. 'Neighbour, see? Because that is what we are to one another. And we'll decide about sending a little message to your mother when you come in, ducky pet. She'd like it. Mr Jackson can take it. He goes that way to work.'

Rosa hurried down the stairs clutching the authorization form in one hand and a red bean mooncake in the other. She was so relieved she even called out a cheery greeting to Sunday. But he didn't bother to respond.

Sunday the Mediator

Sunday prayed and prayed until the image of a suitable aunt figure came to him. He did not actually see any face but he knew who she must be. He must locate her and speak to her directly. He followed Rosa to school, at a discreet distance. He was practised at moving stealthily through the scrub. This townscape however was harder. The roads were so straight and lacking enough vegetation or tall grasses with which to blend. However, he successfully trailed her all the way to the street on which stood the school without her becoming aware of his presence.

From an observation point behind a red cylindrical mailbox, he watched her skip towards the gates to be surrounded by six or seven other children, all chirruping like crickets in the sun. He saw a girl take hold of Rosa's hand.

That, he surmised, must surely be Jules whom Rosa had said was her true and ever okay loyal friend. But then another child clasped Rosa's other hand. And another came over and laid an arm across Rosa's shoulder, enveloping her and the two others in a casual circle of companionship.

A bell clanged from inside the school. A young woman leaned into the group to hand one of the girls a small backpack. She kissed the child briefly on the cheek, and walked away. The children were scurrying towards the building and lining up. The gates were closing.

Sunday loped quickly alongside the school fence and caught up with the woman.

'Madam. Please excuse me, could you be the mother of Jules?'

'Jules? Oh no. Me, I'm Miriam's sister. If it's Jules you want you ought to speak to her mum. That's her, getting into that car. The blue one.'

Sunday saw the little car move off. He knew how to run. He ran, making no attempt at invisibility. The traffic-lights changing to orange helped him catch up, but then they changed to green and he had to run some more. He finally saw the blue car moving into a multistorey car-park. He followed it through the ticket barrier and up the ramp.

He gave her time to descend from her car, to gather up her shopping bags, to lock her car, while he waited respectfully at a distance beside a concrete pillar near the pedestrians' exit before he stepped out.

'Excuse me, madam,' he said.

She looked terrified.

'If you are the mother of Jules, please may I speak with you? It is a matter of some urgency.'

Harvest Festival

Rosa's first crop, and last, was the radishes. Nothing seemed to be happening in the earth until, after a few sunny days, the tiny green leaflets suddenly appeared. Furtively, they'd been germinating. Below the leaves, soon appeared the red swelling bellies.

She and Enzo gathered all seventeen of them. Proudly, they took them in to show to Sunday. 'See here is just right for us three to feast like the king. Five for each and two more for you for you are biggest.'

'Would we be kinder to save them for this evening?' Sunday suggested. The residents had planned an informal get-together to bid one another farewell.

Rosa said, 'But if too many people are here, then we eat less radish.'

'Have less, share more.'

'Huh, you the boss. If you say, we do it,' said

Rosa, resigned. 'So, Enzo, you do come too, to the celebration?'

Enzo nodded.

'Okay-dokay. Then see you soon,' she said. She went up to 11-N, to wash the radishes. Then her face and hands. She also tidied her hair and carefully packed her things into a black plastic bin-bag. She went down to wait for the event to start, resolving in her own mind that it was not about farewells but to celebrate the success of her garden.

At first there was nobody except for Sunday and herself. But then two men ambled shyly up. Rosa wasn't pleased to see them. They'd done little to help clear the site, nor had they donated plants or useful items.

'They, Mr Aziz, Mr Osman, not even lifted the little finger!' she muttered to Sunday. 'Now they here to feast with the radish and take up our fun.'

Sunday said, 'Rosa, do you not remember how we said the garden would be for young and old, industrious or slothful, of whatever colour or creed? In a paradise garden there is no evil-thinking and no segregation.'

Rosa didn't remember them saying that. 'Huh,' she said. Then, 'Okay, ducky. I geddit. All share. All care.

Be kind.' And she led Mr Osman round her modest plantation, explaining where the sunflower seeds had gone in, and where the beans, though there was unfortunately nothing to show for either sowing.

Meanwhile, Sunday, with the help of Mr Aziz, built a tidy bonfire of dry rubbish which would burn without making a stink.

The Ragazzi brothers turned up. Pacco was scowling. 'Only here to keep an eye on the littl'uns,' he said. Sunday asked if he'd help feed the fire. Pacco tossed items right into the blaze and his scowl changed to a grin. He retrieved two planks that had been destined for the fire. He and Sunday set them up across three newly dumped fridges to provide rough seating.

More people were gathering. Every new arrival brought a contribution. Sunday and Pacco had to improvise a table from an old door, on which to place the accumulating banquet. Mrs Papaconstantinou had a bag of pink and white marshmallows. Mrs Wieczerzak brought a dish of hot potato pancakes rolled up with apple and sour cream inside. Mr McLeod brought a slab of whisky tablet and a frightening curl of black pudding. There were also cheese straws, samosas, mini pizzas, and corn kenkeys.

Mr and Mrs Hamid came staggering up the road,

each carrying several cartons of crisps, cashew nuts, tortilla chips and milk chocolate fingers. The 8-to-late was closing for ever. Mr Hamid would be returning with his wife to the village of his birth which he had not seen since he was fifteen years old. 'So, all our stock must go,' he said triumphantly as he and Mrs Hamid unpacked the cartons on to the table.

The Singh family, and the Khans, formerly of 13-W and 7-E, had already been moved to the Springfield Estate on the far side of town. They arrived in a hired minivan. Jazz Khan drove. Mr Singh unloaded a gas-powered barbecue. Mrs Singh made chapattis and warmed the naan breads. Mrs Khan had prepared a cauldron of tarka dhal which she ladled on to banana-leaf dishes.

Rosa was swept up in the mood of generosity. Eagerly, she sliced the seventeen radishes into halves, then into quarters so everybody could receive a token taste. Enzo solemnly handed the radish slivers round.

'Ah, I bite into the peppery succulence and marvel at the greenness of your fingers,' said Mr Hamid with a wink.

Everybody managed to find something positive to say about their tiny sample of radish, except for Mr

McLeod who pointed out that his sliver had been attacked by wireworm.

Mrs Ndebele turned on him. 'Trust you to complain, you old moaner. How about a compliment for a change?'

Mr McLeod tottered towards her. Mrs Ndebele looked ferocious as a dragon. She clasped her flowery umbrella like a sword. Rosa was afraid they were going to fight. But to her surprise, Mr McLeod stretched out his arms and hugged the old woman. The behaviour of British adults was still difficult to predict.

'Aye, I ken you are right, as usual, Mrs Ndebele. And I'm nae mair than a glaikit old fool. Tis a miracle the lassie made anything at all from yon clarty midden. And tis indeed a fine way to conclude her stay here.'

Then he linked arms with Mrs Ndebele and she linked with Mrs Wieczerzak and she with one of the Singhs until there was a circle of old people. The sun was sinking in a rose-pink glow beyond the railway tracks. Mr McLeod began to sing.

'Well I'll be blessed,' said Mrs Ndebele. 'If it's not the Auld Lang Syne!'

She and several of the elderly folk seemed to know the words or at least the tune and were swinging their linked arms up and down in time. At the end of the song, Mr McLeod wept and had to be helped to a place on the bench.

The Ragazzi brothers tried everything that was spread on the door-top. It was almost as if they hadn't eaten in weeks. Mrs Papaconstantinou showed Rosa and the boys how to thread marshmallows on sticks to toast in the embers of the fire. Eating charred sugar without burning your lips was a challenge.

Jazz Singh fetched the tabla from the van. He beat rhythms that began soft and grew stronger. The Ragazzi brothers began to prance around the glowing fire like captives released. Several of the younger grown-ups joined the dancing. Ms Sardini swayed with the tempo, gently so as not to wake the baby sleeping on her shoulder.

Rosa watched but was not in a mood for dancing. Sunday came and rested his hand on her shoulder. 'This is a fine achievement and you can be filled with righteous pride.'

Rosa nodded. 'But also I have the sorry wishing for my Lila is here.'

Sunday said, 'She is with us in spirit. She may watch the blaze of this fire from her bed.'

'How does she know?'

'I forewarned her of the beacon. I advised her to

look this way as dusk fell.'

Mrs Ndebele, on the bench beside Mr McLeod, suddenly raised her arms in the air and called out how she thanked the Lord that the late Mr Ndebele was no longer at her side. 'For this gala is too good to share with any but the finest of citizens.'

Rosa whispered to Sunday, 'This woman is curious as the cat. All every times, she like telling to me Mr Ndebele is the bad man. But why she will not forget him in her mind but will speak of him again and again?'

Sunday said, 'One day, when we have grown old, the young people of that era will certainly find our behaviour as strange.'

'I will never be strange,' said Rosa firmly. 'That is for sure as boots.'

It wasn't only Mr McLeod and Rosa who felt doleful. Mrs Khan and Mrs Hamid were now exchanging tearful embraces. Mr Jackson and Mr Brown were patting each other on the back and shaking their heads. Sadness was drifting in the air with the smoke. Rosa's sorrow was sharpened by apprehension.

She spotted the small blue car bouncing up the road. Jules and her mother were late. Rosa was glad about that. They were coming to fetch her away and Rosa wasn't sure she wanted to leave. Just as you got used to a place, it was time to move on. Change was so unsettling.

Adieu, Addio, Arrivederci, Odabo, Namaste, Yantoomir, Khudaa Haafiz, Hérete

Jules was out of the car in an instant and scampering through the throng. She reached Rosa's side, jumping up and down like a battery-operated puppet. 'Wow, Rosa! It's just absolutely so incredible and fantasmick. All these people! I thought you were fibbing. But you really do have loads and loads and loads of friends!'

Sunday hurried over with the last of the toasted marshmallows for Jules. Rosa introduced them. 'This Sunday, the good friend.'

'How do you do,' said Sunday with polite formality, as though he had not known who Jules was. There was no reason to clarify who had initiated the fostering arrangement.

Jules wolfed down the marshmallows, then explained

to Sunday, 'Rosa's coming to stay with us. Till her mum's better. Isn't it so so fantastic?'

'This is excellent,' said Sunday gravely, as though it was news.

'And so we're going to be like sisters from now on, aren't we, Rosie-Posie?'

'Yes,' said Rosa. 'This will be okay for us.'

'She's really going to love it at our place. I promised Mum I'll always be nice to her and I'll let her borrow anything of mine she wants, so long as she asks first.'

'Thank you,' said Rosa. 'You are kind.'

Sunday said, 'I am glad that you have come in time to witness this gathering, Jules. For here you see what was God's first intention.' He held out both hands to indicate the crowd. 'We see many peoples from all corners of the globe speaking together in contentment. And so it should have been throughout history if Eve had not introduced the possibility of sin.'

Jules sniggered. 'What's he on about?'

But Rosa knew that when Sunday started speaking of things he read in his ragged old book, it was best not to interrupt.

'If the Lord God, Creator of all, looks down upon us now, surely He will behold a new paradise in the making.'

'Except for the rubbish everywhere,' said Jules, wrinkling her nose. 'It's a bit of a tip, this place.'

Sunday said, 'When His divine glance falls on those rusting fridges, He will see them with the eye of eternity for was it not He who devised the science of refrigeration and the mystery of the oxidation of iron?'

Jules shrugged. 'Whatever.' She whispered to Rosa, 'Mum's friend says he ought to be on legal aid.'

'What's that?'

'Dunno. But they say he definitely ought to apply for it.' And she scampered off to inspect the food on the makeshift table to see what was left.

Mrs Wieczerzak and Mr McLeod, recovering on one of the benches, moved up to make a space for Jules's mother. She was handed a serving of dhal on a banana-leaf dish with a warmed naan bread. Mrs Ndebele shuffled along the bench to sit right next to her.

'You'll find she's a very tidy little madam. Always washes her own socks in the evening and sees to her own hair in the morning,' she said.

Jules's mother glanced doubtfully at the sloppy dhal. She wondered how to eat it without causing offence. There did not seem to be any cutlery. She did her best, scooping up the dahl with a torn-off piece of naan bread.

'Will you try some of this potato pancake?' said Mrs Wieczerzak.

'Or mebbe a piece of this tablet?' said Mr McLeod.

'And you'll also find she's not a fussy eater at all.' Mrs Ndebele went on with her childcare instructions, ignoring the speakers on either side. 'Though she is not so keen on sago.'

'Sago pudding?' said Jules's mother, surprised. 'I didn't know anybody still made that.'

'Then you'll not need to bother with it now,' said Mrs Ndebele. 'But she does love a five-spice dumpling.'

The Singhs and the Khans piled their things back into the hired van. Mr McLeod said, 'Time for a wee bit of heid-back now for the auld folks.' He went to say goodbye to Sunday, shaking his hand again and again. 'You've been a braw laddie. And I wish you the best. And when you're wanting assistance with your application forms, you ken where to find me. But be mindful that the millstones of the Home Office grind exceedingly slow. So dinnae you attend any rapid miracle.'

Mr Aziz and Mr Osman started the clear-up. Pacco,

Martino and Enzo rushed to help. Pacco and Martino raked over the hot embers of the fire. Enzo sprinkled on water from a tin can. Rosa gathered up the banana-leaf plates and dropped them into the composting bin.

Jules watched. She said, 'So what's going to happen to those boys then?'

'Och, dinnae fash yersel on their account,' said Rosa.

'What?' said Jules.

'Now they have own WSW, nice good man. He take them to nice Home to live and soon find their uncles.'

Jules pointed at Sunday. 'And *him*, your not-boyfriend? Where's *he* going?'

Rosa, too, had wondered. 'He will not say me. He will say, never your business affair, Miss Nosy.'

'It won't be much fun for him here if everybody else is leaving. Maybe he should come down to our place. Mum wouldn't mind, not if she's already got you. He could probably sleep in our garage.'

Rosa did not think that sleeping in a garage would be any better than sleeping in a storeroom.

Jules said, 'He'd be fine in the daytime. He might have to hide after six when the neighbours next door get in from work. Mum says they're a bit funny about immigrants from overseas.'

'How is funny? You know I am the immigrant too.'

'Yes, but you're different. It's the others, the dark ones. They say it causes negative equity. Whatever that is.'

Rosa's apprehension increased. Negative equity did not sound promising.

The party was definitely over. The fire was well and truly out. The sun had gone. The yellow glow from the ring-road lighting had taken over.

Jules's mother said, 'Have you got your things ready, dear?'

Rosa nodded. Everything she owned was in the bin-bag, in the Hawk Rise entrance hall.

'Well then,' said Jules's mother. 'We better be off. Early start for school tomorrow.'

'Not early for Rosa,' said Jules brightly. 'It'll be more like a lie-in for her. She used to have to get up at quarter to seven, didn't you?'

Rosa nodded but was too exhausted to say anything useful.

One week after the radish harvest, the construction workers arrived. Three flat-bed trucks with hoists drew up in the parking bay. Before Sunday had pulled himself out of his sleeping bag, breeze blocks, scaffolding poles, a diesel-powered generator and a cement mixer were being unloaded and stacked in an orderly manner on top of paradise. The workforce erected a chain-link fence, three metres tall, topped with razor wire, around the whole of the Hawk Rise site. Then they made the equipment and machines secure and went away for several weeks.

Wonderland

It was mysterious to inhabit Hawk Rise now that it was silent. Sunday managed, nonetheless, to rejoice in his heart that all former residents had been successfully rehoused. Every single member of his flock now had a place to lay their head. Some still had uncertainty concerning their legal status. However, as Sunday understood it, those, like Ms Sardini and Mr Aziz, whose long-term future in The Wonderland was on hold, had been offered a representative to guide them through the maze.

Now, he must regularize his own situation. He was hopeful of the outcome. Jules's mother had been hopeful. Mr Hamid had been hopeful. The Ragazzi boys' WSW had been helpful as well as hopeful and had told Sunday of an organization that supported young, unaccompanied asylum seekers. He offered to make the first phone call on Sunday's behalf.

But Sunday resolved to see what he could achieve with the information he had already gleaned. Mr McLeod had suggested he present himself at the Citizens Advice Bureau. He would do that first.

Three years back, when Mr McLeod was fully mobile, the Citizens Advice Bureau had indeed been a hub of positive citizenship. But Mr McLeod was now an old fellow, out of touch and unaware that the levelling of Hawk Rise to create a leisure centre and shopping mall was only the tip of an iceberg of improvements. The whole town was undergoing a programme of regeneration.

When Sunday located the former advice bureau, he found it to be an outlet for the trade of second-hand garments.

How could he not clap his hands in joy that disabled youngsters would benefit from the funds raised? He returned to Hawk Rise undaunted.

He was no further in his own quest for life security. But he would persevere. To whom should he next turn for advice?

He opened his bible at the Book of Exodus and the answer came to him quickly. Pharaoh's daughter had received a destitute child to bring up as her own. She was a good woman. The mother of Jules had, in similar fashion, received a destitute child, Rosa, to care for her as her own. She too was a good woman.

Where did she live? In the time of Moses and his adoptive grandfather, the Pharaoh, it was easier to locate people's abodes.

It was late afternoon when Sunday reached the school. The children had long since left. The main doors were closed. He saw movement in a side room. A woman was sorting papers by a filing cabinet. He tapped on the window. She looked up, surprised. She came to the window and opened it. Sunday did not wish to seem like a desperate vagrant. He tried to explain his situation calmly and why he needed the address of Jules's family.

As patiently as she heard out pupils' accounts of lost mittens, nicked notebooks and extraordinarily dramatic domestic incidents, she now listened to Sunday's tale.

'No, my dear,' she concluded. 'That is definitely not information we release. Unethical is the word. You say you're a family friend but I don't know you from Adam.'

'Madam, I beseech you.'

She said, 'No, dear, please don't do that. Now, I don't know much about immigration legislation, but there's a centre in town where you might well find somebody to help you out.' She wrote an address on a slip of paper and passed it through the window.

'Madam, I thank you.'

'Best of luck.'

The Visitors

Rosa had become such a hungry reader. She and Jules had to visit the library twice a week, on Saturdays and Wednesdays.

'More fun for you than me,' said Jules. 'But it gets me out of Mum's hair.'

On their way home on Wednesday, Jules announced they would make a detour.

'Where to detour?'

'To find your pal. Check up on him. You'd like that, wouldn't you?'

'Whatever.' So much more expressive than okay-dokay. 'But maybe and maybe he's not there.'

'Well, we won't know till we get there, will we?'

They found the Hawk Rise site fenced off. They saw the building materials stacked but no sign of building or demolition work. They saw notices warning them to keep out, informing them that all entry was prohibited, that it was a dangerous site. Jules found a gap low down in the chain-link fence.

'No!' said Rosa.

Jules crawled through anyway.

'Please. You can be hurt. Come back. Anything can happen.'

''Course it won't.'

Jules trotted up to the front of the building. The entrance door was boarded over. 'ENTRY PROHIBITED' said a sign. Jules pressed her face to the boarding. She roared at the top of her voice, 'Sunday, you in there? We've come to see you.'

There was no reply. She walked back, crawled under the fence. She said, 'Rosa, listen, you better leave him a note.'

Rosa said, 'He's not here.'

'Even if he isn't in there right now, he might come back just to look at it, same as us. If you're not going to do it, I am.' She tore a half-page out of her Creative Writing notebook.

Hi Sunday. Where R U?!!! Rosa wants to know. Mum (Jules mum) says if U haven't got a place yet U come and stop over at ours in the spare-

room. Mum says shes got a yoga friend who works in a soliciters office and can give U gd advice if you want!!!!!
Take care and LOL (lots of love) Rosa and Jules.
PS we will come back next Wednesday afternoon!!!!

Jules said, 'Now we better run for it or else Mum's going to ask why we took so long.'

Rosa was glad to get away. Seeing the place again made her sad.

Shelter

Sunday found the location which the school secretary had recommended. A group of men were gathering on the steps. Some sitting. Some shuffling. Some standing. Most were smoking. Some smelled of alcohol. Sunday stepped through them to read the notice on the main door. It said that inside, swearing, weapons, alcohol would not be tolerated.

'Oy, oy, you boyo! Mind your manners. No barging. First come, first served.'

Sunday went back to the end of the queue. The building was a night shelter for the homeless. At six, the doors opened and the men flowed in.

The men were given hot soup, bread, numbered tickets for their beds and a metal token for use of the showers. Sunday asked the man in charge of the soup cauldron if he could ask for some guidance on a legal matter.

'I'm only a volunteer, mate. Your advisory team's here in the morning, eight sharp.' The man reeled off the services the hostel would provide. 'Healthcare, entitlement to benefits, chiropody, dentistry, tracing missing family. Mental welfare. Substance misuse group.'

'Thank you.'

'You're welcome. Access to the dormitories is from seven o'clock. Got your ticket okay? Well done.'

The men cleared away their soup dishes, watched television, played dominoes. Mostly they talked. Even without the encouragement of drink, their voices increased in loudness. They held shouted conversations with several people at once, right across the room. Sunday was accustomed to the quiet. This clamour was intolerable. He tried to withdraw into his own private space but could not. He was in a madhouse. He felt that he would lose his mind.

It was said that God had made all men in His own image. Yet how could this be so? Here was the shabby residue of humanity. And Sunday knew himself to be furthest of any from a reflection of God's golden radiance. He was not worthy of a place here.

He had to get out. At ten minutes to nine,

overwhelmed with despair, he left the hostel just before the volunteer closed the doors for the night.

He made his way back to Hawk Rise. He passed crimson devils fighting in dark corners. Overhead, he saw the bright streaks of angels skimming across the sky, but none of them reached down for him.

He drew apart the double rows of spiked wire, crawled under the chain-link fence, pulled aside the broad sheet of chipboard that covered the entrance and slunk back into the familiarity of his tomb.

The Sanctuary

Through the air vent, Sunday detected familiar weather, overcast sky with light drizzle, similar to his first day in The Wonderland. He waited calmly. Who would reach him first? The Prophet of the Lord Almighty or the personnel from immigration?

Who would care for living like a rat in a dark hole? He had wanted to move. But to where? Not back to the madhouse hostel. Not to sleep on a layer of cardboard in a shop doorway. Besides, those benefits interrogators that Mrs Wieczerzak had set on him insisted he should make no change of address without informing them.

He would have liked to have a wash so as to be fresh to greet them. But the water supply to Hawk Rise had long since been disconnected. The electricity too. He wiped his face, hands and feet with a dry rag. He would have appreciated a sustaining mug of hot soup made from one of the pour-and-stir packets Mr Hamid had left. But the camping gas cylinder was empty.

He drained the last drops of Tropical Fruit Juice from the carton. Before leaving, so many people had been so kind, had given him much that they could not afford to give away. For a while, his storeroom had been almost like Mr Hamid's shop, except that here he was the sole customer.

He did not know if he would be fed once he was in custody. So he took a slice of the floppy white bread lurking at the bottom of its plastic bag. He trimmed off the blue crusts. He spread it with all the marmalade that was left in the jar.

'Oxford English Marmalade. Thick cut. Made to traditional recipe.'

He had never got to Oxford, seat of the oldest university in the world after Uppsala. He had never made it to anywhere in The Wonderland other than Lowestoft and here.

He tried to whisper the words of grace before he ate his bread.

Above him were the seventeen storeys, four flats to a storey, every one of them now vacant. Meanwhile, scattered across other regions of The Wonderland were one hundred thousand homeless families. In the centre of this town, men without homes slept in the hostel dormitories with the coughing and shouting of nightmares all around them. In other cities, men and women slept in alleyways. If only they could be rehoused here. But after the building had been cordoned off, a notice had been attached to the main door declaring Hawk Rise unfit for human habitation. This was indeed what Sunday had felt when he had first entered. Only over time, did one learn how it was not the quality of the construction but the quality of the people which rendered a place habitable.

Sunday was the only human left, though other creatures were still resident. Mites in the crevices, millipedes in the dry sink, silver fish scurrying after dark when he caught the glint of their scales.

Sunday's loss of faith had been a brief error on his part. Before it grew too dark to see, he looked up the daily reading. It was from the Gospel according to St Matthew, a passage familiar to Sunday. 'You have heard that it was said, You shall love your neighbour and hate your enemy. But I say to you, love your enemies.'

He closed his bible. He ripped long strips from the covering of his sleeping bag. With them, he bound the book firmly to his torso, just as when he had set out on his journey.

It was unlikely he would be permitted to take personal items with him. If Mr Aziz was to be believed, the authorities believed that every smuggled-in or escorted-out person carried drugs or bombs. If the book was confiscated, at least he knew enough of it by heart should he ever need it. And the book might fall into the hands of someone who would benefit. Whatever happened to him, he would be ready.

The minutes passed. The hours passed. Then the days. Perhaps even the weeks. He did not know how long he had been waiting. He did not know the season. His spirit was so low that he forgot to pray. He had been forgotten by all who had offered to help him. He had neglected God. God punished him by forgetting him.

Controlled Excitement

All across town, former residents of Hawk Rise prepared for the strange event. In Sunnysides residential home, Mr McLeod explained to the young woman who brought round the mid-morning tea trolley the finer details of how the destruction was to be carried out.

He had forgotten that he had already told her several times. She had not forgotten.

'That's right, Angus, pet,' Heather agreed. 'A special team of demolition experts, some of them coming all the way up from Devizes.'

'And the explosive. Did I tell you who invented the dynamite?'

'Indeed you did, Angus. A Swedish engineer, Alfred Nobel.'

'Who made such a bonny penny he set up the

Nobel peace prize?'

'That's right, Angus. So you said.'

'Aye, and safer than nitroglycerine which can be dangerously unstable.'

Heather marvelled how these old folk could retain facts from the long gone past, yet often failed to recall the name of a familiar visitor from one day before.

'And you also told me, Angus, how the invention was intended exclusively for commercial blasting and other peaceful purposes.'

'Fegs, if you are such an erudite lassie, why are you footering your time looking after old poops like us? You should be teaching history in high school.'

'Because this is what I'm trained for, Angus.'

'If you are trained for it, you'll mind to call me Mr McLeod and show a bit of respect.'

Heather smiled and moved on with the tea trolley to the next resident. The Sunnysides manager came through to the day room to say that Angus's taxi was here.

Meanwhile, in her self-contained flat in the warden-assisted housing complex known as Green Glades, Mrs Ndebele put a final touch of varnish to her fingernails which would be much in view when her hand pressed the detonator button. Hibiscus scarlet nails would distract the public's gaze from her knobbly knuckles. As a girl she had had hands as soft as lilies, that's what Billy had said.

Mrs Ndebele had been selected for the honourable task as she was believed to have been the first-ever resident to move into Hawk Rise. Mrs Wieczerzak, now residing down the road at Silverlawns, tried to claim that she was the first tenant but she, in Mrs Ndebele's opinion, was losing her memory. The old fusser, Mr McLeod, had also wanted to do the detonating. He said it was a man's job and he knew about explosives.

'I don't need to know about the explosives, ducky,' Mrs Ndebele had told him when they met at the Third Age Horticultural Club. 'I just have to be there on time, and do what they tell me. It's all electronicified. But if I get it wrong, it'll be good to know you're there to lend a hand.'

Mrs Ndebele understood that her role was merely symbolic. Nonetheless, she felt a shiver of apprehension. This would be the second time in her life that she had watched her home destroyed. As a young girl she had seen the attap thatch of the neighbours' house burning, then the attap of her own home catch alight. By dawn, the whole row of houses had been levelled to smouldering ash. Her childhood home, one storey tall, had been built upon a stilted wooden platform over a saltwater swamp. This time, there would be seventeen storeys of concrete, breeze blocks and iron girders to come down.

At Jules's home, they were preparing to leave for school when Jules asked her mother, for the second time, if they couldn't please please have the day off. Her mother's response was predictable.

'Don't be silly. Of course not. You have to go to school.'

'Oh Mum, you're such a party-pooper. It's Rosa's home they're blowing up. She *needs* to be there for her memory store.'

'Temporary home,' her mother corrected her. 'And only for a relatively short time. It's not like she was born there.'

'But Mum. Rosa really wants to go. Don't you, Rosie-Posie?'

'Perhaps,' said Rosa carefully. 'If it is convenient.'

Jules's mother gave Rosa an apologetic hug. 'Sorry, my dear. But I wouldn't be seen as much of a foster-mum if I let you bunk off every time Jules had one of her bright ideas. And if we're not seen to be taking proper care of you, the foster officer might decide to move you somewhere else.'

Jules stuck her chin out and grunted.

Rosa said politely, 'No worries. And it is nice here, very nice. Everything is considerably nice and my mamma says always you are some very nice kind English people.'

Jules's mother said, 'That's the spirit. Positive thinking. And we'll probably catch something about it on the local news this evening. I'll make you a really nice tea. Any special requests, either of you?'

There weren't. Rosa ate what she was offered. Jules said she didn't care.

In class, Jules asked their teacher if she and Rosa could have leave of absence for half an hour to go up to Hawk Rise. 'It'll be quite safe,' she added knowingly, 'because it's all going to be supervised destruction.'

Ms Martin did not consider this a valid excuse for missing lessons.

'But it's historic, miss,' Jules pleaded.

'First I have heard of that,' said Ms Martin. 'I doubt your mother would think much of the idea either.'

Naturally, Jules didn't reveal that she'd already tried her mother twice. Jules was disappointed. Rosa was not. Life was working out okay-dokay. She didn't want to risk any upsets in her latest home with its clean socks and kindness every morning. Jules was affectionate though she didn't seem to get it that there might be more to life than pranks and fun.

Rescue Party

Sunday continued to wait in the storeroom in the semi-dark, without water, without electricity, without food. Devils taunted him through the air vent.

'Coming to get you. Coming. Get you. You. Coming. Coming soon,' their voices crowed. But it was not the evil spirits, nor the angels, nor the immigration people who came.

It was the demolition squad who found him when they were checking the building prior to laying the fuses.

'Blimey! What in heck's he doing in here?'

Sunday struggled to his feet. He hadn't expected as many as six men to come for him.

'Damn lucky we found you, mate, or you'd have been a gonna. The whole bangshoot's going up. Didn't you know?'

Sunday stared at them. What were they saying? What did they mean?

'How long you been in there? This ain't no place for playing hide-and-seek.'

Sunday nodded.

'Poor lad's all confused. Disorientated.'

'We better get him out of here.'

One of the men fetched his lunch pack. 'You look hungry, mate. Like a bite to eat?'

'Thank you,' Sunday whispered hoarsely.

The demolition worker opened his lunch box and unwrapped the silver foil round his sandwiches. He handed the pack to Sunday. 'Help yourself.'

Sunday hesitated.

'Don't worry, son. No fear of pork in there. They're all Red Leicester. Wife's made me vegetarian. Thinks it'll help save the world. Take a lot more than everybody giving up sausages to do that, if you ask me.'

Sunday took a cheese sandwich and bit into it. But his throat was so dry he could not swallow. To be offered a working man's lunch and then reject it was so ungracious.

'Look at his eyes. He's dehydrated. You need a drink, man.'

Another of the team fetched the vacuum flask from

his jacket pocket. He poured Sunday a mugful of tea. 'Drink up, sunshine. That'll put a lift in your step.'

The tea was thick and sweet, made with evaporated milk, the way Auntie Pru used to do it. Sunday drank it gratefully. The mug was refilled. And the sandwiches offered again.

These men were kind and thoughtful. When they saw he was cold, one of them took off his own fleece for Sunday to put on. Then their team manager turned up. She wore the same hard hat and uniform overalls but was stern and authoritative.

'How'd he get in?' she demanded. 'What was security up to? I thought this place was supposed to be secure?'

Sunday was too confused to explain that he had once been the caretaker. He blinked as they led him into daylight. The sky was overcast, but brighter than Sunday had seen for some time. He stumbled across the forecourt with them. On the fence he saw something flapping, like a white bird trapped in the wire. It was a scrap of paper. It had his name on it.

Hi!!!! We been to visit you twice, me and Rosa. But you aren't here. This our second time. If you come back get in touch. please!!!!! We MISS

284

you!!!!! Love and hugs, Jules and Rosie-Posie, LOL
XXXXX

It was too late. And he was not worthy of their
friendship.

Journey's End

When Prudence reached her village it was eerily quiet. The handful of other returnees shared a common sadness. They did not speak more than was necessary.

Prudence's hut, like every home in the village, had been vandalized and looted. Even the wooden lintel over the doorway had been stolen. The thatch had been burned. But the mud walls still stood as if guarding her iron bedstead. Two of her tin pans lay in the dust riddled with holes as if used for target practice. Other returning villagers had lost far more. A few had lost less. Returnees shared what they had. Prudence gave thanks to the Almighty for guiding her home to die under the familiar sky.

The blue beret peace-keepers had come and the killers had moved on. Next came the aid-givers. Prudence received a ten-kilo sack of grain, a ten-litre plastic water-carrier. Her roof was securely covered with a sheet of blue plastic to keep out the rains until it could be re-thatched.

Advisors began coming regularly to determine what support to give the village. It would take time and effort to make the place self-sustaining once more.

'I have patience as well as prudence,' Prudence told one of the investigators. The keen young co-workers who brought guarantees of charitable gifts had to make decisions on their distribution. An interviewer, who appeared to Prudence little older than a schoolgirl, arrived, computer in hand, to question Prudence on her age, her health, how many dependents shared her home.

'So you are sorting the sheep from the goats?' Prudence observed. 'You will find I am a very ancient goat, not worth a lot.'

The administrator explained that no sheep were involved. The immediate allocation concerned hens and goats, purchased with money donated by schoolchildren in the far off Wonderland. Prudence was to receive four pullets.

Prudence named the hens and supervised them as carefully as if they were her nieces. Humility, Charity, Mercy and Glory pecked around her feet in the compound. She listened out for them and if they went too far afield, she lured them back with a handful of grain.

Her sight was not improving. The cataract in the left eye gave the world a blurry sheen. The other eye had been infected by grit on the journey. But she would not call herself blind. She was not like her neighbour, Ebenezer, who had been sightless even as a child. Yet had he not managed well enough for sixty years? And now his spirit had been lifted by the unexpected reappearance of his grandson. The boy was quieter than he used to be, hardly spoke a word, but was alive.

Morning and evening, Prudence continued to pray for her own dear boy, that he might be keeping in good health and keeping good company. She must not pray for his return. That was asking too much of the Lord who had more than enough on His plate with the people still in the camp.

When, sometimes, Prudence found herself regretting that she had ever encouraged her only surviving relative to leave the camp, she suppressed that thought. It was not profitable. How could she have predicted then that the situation here might improve to such an extent? Only the angels and the Holy Trinity could see the past, present and future. Mortals must make do with the constrictions of earthly time span.

In the Control Room of Destruction

Sunday's rescuers took him to their Portakabin which stood on the ground where the broken climbing-frame used to be. Inside it was like a laboratory. Monitors were blinking. Desks were spread with charts. Keyboards clicked and electric circuits whirred.

One of the team gave Sunday a cup of coffee. Another showed him a chair in the corner where he was out of their way. He sipped quietly, listening to the team discussions. Auntie Pru used to say, 'It is by listening that we may learn.'

Sunday heard them speak of velocity, high brisance, inert desensitizers, detonator initiators, booster charges and so many things which he did not understand.

When he had first heard from Mr McLeod that Hawk Rise had an incurable building sickness and was to be taken down, he supposed this would be achieved methodically, storey by storey, so that the windows, doors, floors and other materials might be reused. Now, by listening to these experts, he discovered that they were not intending to take the tower down but to blow it up. They would not be starting from the top but from strategic points on the ground floor and within the lift shaft.

Despite the devastation under discussion, the atmosphere inside the Portakabin was calm. He had been cold and fearful of the future for too long. Now he was warm and safe amongst these gentle people. It was a relief not to have to pretend any more. His future was not his to control. The quiet murmur of their incomprehensible conversations, the regular flutter of their monitor screens, lulled Sunday into a semi-conscious daze. It was a relief not to have to wait any more. His future was not his to determine.

The Memorial Mango

The tree was still in the compound, though not as she had left it. It had been reduced to a stump, rough and blackened on one side where the rogues had lit a fire at the base.

Prudence fingered it over as carefully as a nurse with a serious burns patient. It was not dead. The sap was still rising. It still had one limb and on that limb was a shoot so small it might seem insignificant.

Not to her. She would tend this war victim, encourage its recovery, just as the aid-bringers were supporting the restoration of the village. She planned to do more than encourage regrowth. Once the hens had begun laying so she had eggs to sell, she would buy the tree a companion, another mango but of a different variety. She would make a trip to the Agricultural Research and Development Station. She would seek advice from the horticulturalists. Highly trained young men and women were being deployed to the region to rebuild the economy as well as the homes. They would know the best species to plant for this soil.

And if the old mango survived, she would cherish it, not for its meagre crop of stringy fruit, but as a reminder of all that had taken place in this compound, the good and the bad. It would be a memorial to those who once sat in its shade and who rested now, and for all eternity, in the majestic halls of paradise.

The Truants

At breaktime Jules wore one of her determined expressions. She cornered Rosa in the playground. Rosa knew she must be plotting a new dodge.

'Our superiors,' Jules whispered like a spy conveying information, 'have totally failed to recognize the emotional and historical significance of today's key event. We must take the matter into our own hands.'

'You saying, dearie, we bunk off?'

'It's called showing initiative. It's an important event in your life. You need to be there. So I'm going to be your secret facilitator.'

Jules led Rosa round the perimeter of the juniors' playground towards the service gates where they were out of sight of the playtime assistant. The gates were kept locked to prevent undesirable intruders. You just had to know the code for the keypad. Jules did.

Jules knew plenty about the world. Rosa did too. But the things they knew were different. That's why they could lend the help-hand to each other with their class topics.

'If anybody asks, we say we're running an errand.'

'This is not true.'

'Okay then, if anybody asks if you've got permission, you say, Yes, because I am giving you permission. Now you must give me permission.'

Rosa nodded. 'Give the permission.'

Jules went through the gate first, rapidly. Rosa followed. Jules started running.

'Stop!' Rosa said. 'To hurry makes attention on us. We walk with carelessness. Like this.'

So then they ambled down the road, speeding up once they were two streets distant from school. But soon Jules began to moan she was totally tired. 'Can't walk any more. It's been miles. My legs are knackered.'

'You are the wee daftie,' said Rosa. 'Sure you have the legs to walk.' She didn't have to remind Jules that she used to walk it every day, both ways.

Others were also heading out of town. They had the excited look, as if they were off to a festival in another village. The police people had put up yellow metal signs showing the traffic which way to go. Some of the drivers got mad when they were told to go a different way but the police stayed cheerful as if they were all in a good mood too.

'Emergency services only. Follow the signs for the deviation. This is a potentially dangerous event. Protecting public safety is our number one.'

Jules stopped going on about her tired legs. It was beginning to be exciting for her too. 'Y'know, Rosie-Posie, meeting up with you is the most interesting thing that's ever happened. I'm going to write you up in our topic notebooks.'

'So what you write?'

'Don't know yet.'

'Maybe is better you find some more interesting thing to write. I am just the one small normal person girl.'

'Oh look, Rosie!' Jules cried suddenly. 'Up there!'

Over their heads two air balloons were flying up through the drizzle, higher and higher like gulls in the breeze. Rosa thought, if she was up there, she'd be able to see the whole world spread out. And if Lila was up there, she'd be able to see all the way back to the village with Granpap leaning on the wooden fence, looking up at the clouds and foretelling tomorrow's weather.

Big Bang Delayed

A designated viewing area at a safe distance from the tower block and the Portakabin had been prepared for spectators. Mr McLeod's care assistant, Heather, selected a good position near the podium from where the mayor would deliver his speech. Heather unfolded a camping chair for Mr McLeod. He relished the fussing he received at Sunnysides more than he had expected.

'Heather, lassie. You see yon building? Did you know, I used to bide right there, it used to be my home?'

'Yes, Angus. You told me. And that's why we've come up here to look.'

'There was a gleg laddie looked after us. Said he was fra' the Netherlands but I ken he was from further afield. I gave him my number at Sunnysides. But he's never called, has he?'

'No, Angus. Your friend hasn't called.'

'I'd have liked to help the lad a wee bit more. But with the move, I was trauchled. Culture shock they call it. It mebbe slipped my mind.'

Heather patted his shoulder. 'He'll be fine, your young friend, I'm sure he will. Don't you worry. Now, let's relax and enjoy the spectacle.'

The wait was becoming prolonged. Mr McLeod grew restless.

'The dignitaries have yet to arrive,' said Heather, whose hearing was better than Mr McLeod's so she'd caught the announcement from the loudspeakers. 'The bigwigs from the council offices.'

'Earwigs off the sick orifices?' said Mr McLeod.

'Yes. We have to wait till they get here. They've been held up by the traffic deviations.'

'Ah, the affirmations. Good,' said Mr McLeod.

Others in the crowd also grew bored of hanging about behind a barrier while nothing happened. Some gave up their positions at the front and wandered off to take refreshments from the enterprising Kurdish hot-dog seller who had pushed his trolley all the way up from the multistorey car-park.

Sunday, who was seated inside the Portakabin,

was in position for one of the best views of all. He was startled out of his daze when the thirty-minute countdown on the monitor screens began.

At the safety barrier, Mr McLeod explained to two women with toddlers in buggies the nature of controlled peacetime blasts. 'It's as well ye should know what to expect. So yon bairns will nae be afeart. Technically, an explosion is not what we are here to witness. It will be an implosion. That is, if those ordnance laddies have done their job as they should. They'll have laid the explosives to cause the tower to collapse in upon itself. Do ye understand me?'

'Sssh,' said one of the mothers. 'The mayor's about to speak.'

The mayor, panting, climbed on to the podium and took the microphone. He made a speech about progress and regeneration.

Jules and Rosa wormed their way through the crowd towards the barrier. 'Hey, Rosie-Posie, see what I brought with me,' said Jules.

'What?'

'Mum's camera. Digital.'

'You stole it? Oh crikey mikey, that is really no good.' Rosa still liked living at Jules's home. But she found some of the things Jules did rather odd.

'Only borrowed. She's lent it me before. Look, it's brilliant, got all these features. Anti-blue technology, don't know what that is. Face detection. So you can spot your friends, I guess. Dust reduction system. Dead useful. Bound to be loads of dust. And wobble technology. That'll be handy. This whole place is going to wobble like crazy.'

'Maybe like the earthquake?'

Jules said, 'Hey, there's that man in a funny hat-thingy looking at you. From your party. He's coming over.'

It was Mr Hamid. He edged his way over to them. 'Good day, Rosa. This is a pleasure to see you again.'

'And I am over the moon to see you,' Rosa said. 'This is my friend Jules.'

Mr Hamid nodded. 'I remember meeting you at the farewell.'

Jules said, 'And she's living with me now. She's my foster-sister.'

Mr Hamid beamed. 'Indeed, I recall the arrangement being negotiated. And you certainly look well, Rosa. And such fine command of language. When you first arrived, you could hardly utter a single word! And your mother, is doing well?'

'Better all the time,' said Jules. 'We go and visit her on Saturdays before library time.'

'And are you studying well?'

Rosa shrugged.

Jules said, 'You bet she is. Always top. Billions of Endeavour stars. And she's captain of the netball team. And treasurer of school garden club.'

Mr Hamid said, 'I have already greeted several of your former neighbours from the tower block. But I have not spotted our mutual friend, the young caretaker. Mrs Hamid and I have been so preoccupied with final arrangements for our departure, we have had little time for anything else. But we would like to know what has become of him.'

Jules said, 'Rosa wants to see him too. We've been up here twice looking for him. And Mum came up with a friend too last weekend. She knows someone who could help him with his paperwork.'

'So did you speak with him?' asked Mr Hamid.

'Nope. Rosa said we'd find him here. But we didn't. We couldn't get in. The whole place was already fenced off. Rosa was a bit sad, weren't you, Rosa? But my mum says by now he'll be safe as houses in a children's home. He's only fifteen, you know. Can you believe it! I thought he was a proper grown-up.'

The mayor stepped down from the podium. More hot dogs were sold. The air smelled of frying onions.

Bye-bye Ali Sunday

From her position on the podium, Mrs Ndebele saw a kerfuffle but her sight was not as sharp as it used to be. She could just make out a slim figure of indeterminate gender, in a blue shirt, being led away from the site by two men. She guessed it was probably one of those environment protesters who'd been talking on the local news last evening. The new leisure development wasn't going to be everybody's cup of tea. She certainly wouldn't be coming up here to bathe in a tropical-style pool. Or be pummelled by young men in leotards.

Whatever the fuss was about, the offender was led quickly towards a waiting vehicle.

People from the back of the crowd were surging forward. Rosa and Jules found themselves hemmed in by tall adults so could see little except upwards. Rosa gazed at the sky. Hundreds more air balloons, red and white, were being released. They were advertising the company which was to provide temporary accommodation for the on-site construction workers. Had Rosa noticed Sunday climbing into the back of the van and being driven away she would have wanted to scream and run after the van, but she would have been hindered by the pressing crowd. And whatever she had done, it wouldn't have made any difference.

The deportation officers were not from the Home Office but hired from a private company. They had years and years of expertise in the expulsion of illegals. It could be a curious and unpleasant business, especially when it was women or children they had to deal with. And most especially if the woman resisted, or if she was visibly pregnant and had to be forcibly restrained. Some officers couldn't handle that side of their job.

But the men sent to pick up Piet Ali had grown accustomed to the task and were not distressed by what they had to do. The individual concerned was quite slight. He looked shifty but manageable. He did not struggle. He said, 'Thank you,' when they showed him on to the seat in their vehicle.

Descent of the Hawk

The rain eased off. At last came Mrs Ndebele's big moment. Wearing a hard hat and under close supervision, she placed her hibiscus red fingernail on the detonator button. Nothing happened. It was as if the world held its breath. A baby babbled into the silence.

Mrs Ndebele turned to the director. 'Oh ducky, have I done it wrong?'

The engineer smiled. 'Just wait,' she said quietly and at that moment the mighty tower began to collapse inwards like a penitent falling to his knees.

Rectangular puffs of white smoke burst out through the windows. The crowd gasped. Cameras sparkled and flashed like fireflies. The low boom came after, then another, and another, and with each, the tower sank closer to the ground.

In less than a count from one to ten, it was down in a heap of rubble. The people stood still as rocks, watching the little white window-clouds gather together and expand to form into one large cloud which billowed up like cumulus.

There were one or two tentative handclaps. Then, as the crowd's confidence grew that this was the right thing to do and that something glorious had been achieved, the applause increased and there was cheering too.

Mr McLeod beamed at those nearest him, satisfied that his predictions on management of the implosion had been correct.

The surrounding structures, the railway sidings, the disused warehouses, were undisturbed. The only damage, if it could be called that, was the soft shroud of dust now covering the new cars in the compound. It would rinse off in the next rainstorm.

Truant's Return

Rosa and Jules lurked beside the rear gates of the school until the education authority's recycling van which collected used paper came up. They sidled in alongside it and were back in their places in class just as afternoon register had been called.

Ms Martin raised an eyebrow for their lateness. However, though she deduced from their dusty hair and shoes where they had been, compounding their truancy with disobedience, she did not send them to the Head for punishment. The vulnerable refugee child was finally beginning to lose her hard edge, even to blossom. The achievement of maintaining a friendship with a child of her own age was already a significant step in her rehabilitation. It would be a mistake to destroy that progress.

In Detention

The deportation guards were more severe than the immigration officers. They ordered Sunday to stand, to come here, go there, sit, face the wall, hands on head, feet apart. The change of his minders had been so abrupt. He did whatever they told him to. They called him 'black filth', 'scrounger scum' and other cruder names which made him cringe because they were untrue. His parents had been married when he was born. The colour of his skin had been given him by God. He had taken nothing except another man's name, and even that he had paid money for.

He crouched like a dog in the back of the vehicle which was driving him to the point of departure. He had arrived in The Wonderland unshackled in the back of a truck. He was leaving The Wonderland in the back of a truck, handcuffed and inside a wire cage.

He could no longer pray. His soul was in too dark a place. All the good people he had encountered, all the kindnesses he had received, all the beauty he had seen in the dark cloudy skies, all the faces smiling through the rain, were eroded.

How he hated this country. He hated these people. They had no respect for him. He had none for them. He longed to be anywhere but here. If the guards threatened to kill him, he would tell them he was glad for he could go directly to his Father's Kingdom.

The Roast Beef of Old England

To Jules and Rosa's disappointment, the local news that evening broadcast only a brief report on the demolition of the local landmark. It was followed by a longer report on the latest successful swoop-down on illegals in the region. Central government targets were being met.

By then, Jules's mother had already switched off the television and was serving her daughter and foster-child with a fine meal of roast beef, Yorkshire pudding and roast potatoes. There were also fresh broad beans for Rosa.

As Jules's mother passed the gravy boat down the table she heard an explosive crack. A raw egg had been thrown at their dining-room window. Why would anybody do a thing like that? Not to worry. She would wipe it off after.

Rosa went white as a sheet and could not finish her food.

The Loved One

In the compound by her home, Prudence rested on an upturned plastic crate. She leaned her back against the stump of the tree. As yet, its single bare branch gave no shade. But she was content. Her hens scratched around nearby. That morning, Mercy had laid the first egg. The others would surely soon want to copy her.

The engineers were at work on the old well. It was a noisy business. But worth the racket and the shaking of the ground. Access to clean water was going to be the most significant improvement to this village in a long time. It would improve the villagers' lives for generations to come.

There was a commotion beyond the village perimeter, up on the track. In the bad days, this signalled the arrival of the squads. Time to hide in your home, or run for the thorny scrub. But the calls of the youngsters were cheerful. A boy began to beat a welcome rhythm with a stick on a metal container.

The children had spotted an outline on the horizon, making its way towards the village. At first no more than a dark vertical shape. Not a killer. The killers did not walk alone. They did not walk upright.

The figure was walking down the dip in the track throwing up little puffs of red with every step. Young eyes could identify an approaching figure from a long way off. These days, whoever the visitor was, the girls and boys would run to meet them and find out their business.

Prudence heard Ebenezer call his grandson, 'Who is it? Who is coming?'

But the grandson was already running with the others towards the red dust.

'Who is it?' Ebenezer called again.

'How should I know?' Prudence called back.

They listened to the neighbours.

'Look who it is!' called one.

'Walking, walking.'

For those who could see, the figure outlined in his red cloud grew taller the nearer he drew.

'He is barefoot.'

'He is empty-handed.'

'No, he has something. A bag. What does he carry?'

'He is thin. He has come a long way.'

'Where has he been?'

'He is smiling.'

Prudence knew. She heaved herself upright against the tree-trunk. Humility, Charity, Mercy and Glory scattered as she walked towards the commotion.

'Is that you? Is that really you?' she called.

'Auntie Pru?' he said and she knew him by his voice. 'The Good Lord has seen fit to bring me back to you.'

She said, 'Blessed be the name of the Lord.'